NEW PENGUIN SHAKESPEARE
GENERAL EDITOR: T. J. B. SPENCER
ASSOCIATE EDITOR: STANLEY WELLS

WILLIAM SHAKESPEARE

*

THE TEMPEST

EDITED BY
ANNE BARTON

PENGUIN BOOKS

PENGUIN BOOKS

Published by the Penguin Group
Penguin Books Ltd, 27 Wrights Lane, London W8 5TZ, England
Penguin Putnam Inc., 375 Hudson Street, New York, New York 10014, USA
Penguin Books Australia Ltd, Ringwood, Victoria, Australia
Penguin Books Canada Ltd, 10 Alcorn Avenue, Toronto, Ontario, Canada M4V 3B2
Penguin Books (NZ) Ltd, 182–190 Wairau Road, Auckland 10, New Zealand

Penguin Books Ltd, Registered Offices: Harmondsworth, Middlesex, England

This edition first published in Penguin Books 1968
Reprinted with revised Further Reading 1996
3 5 7 9 10 8 6 4

This edition copyright © Penguin Books, 1968
Introduction and Notes copyright © Anne Righter, 1968
Further Reading copyright © Michael Taylor, 1996
All rights reserved

Set in Ehrhardt Monotype
Printed in England by Clays Ltd, St Ives plc

CONTENTS

INTRODUCTION

The Tempest begins with a storm at sea in which there is nothing apparently of the supernatural or the strange. The enemies are wind, an angry sea, and the rocks of an island, even as they were for the colonists in the *Sea-Adventure* off the coast of Bermuda in 1609. On board Alonso's ship, engagements of speech and personality are abrupt and telling. Antonio and Sebastian, even Gonzalo, seem startled to discover that the Boatswain is at least as much concerned to save his own life as that of his sovereign. The storm cares nothing for the name of King and neither, as the peril of the ship increases, do the sailors. Gonzalo is a counsellor, but in the light of the Boatswain's caustic injunction to him to 'command these elements to silence, and work the peace of the present' (I.1.21-2) the skills of his ordinary life become derisory. Antonio and Sebastian discover that the deference due to them as noblemen and courtiers has suddenly evaporated. They are simply in the way. Gonzalo accepts the situation in which he finds himself with a wry and endearing humour. Antonio and Sebastian have no resource but abuse. Yet for all three of them in this opening scene the normal world of the court, the accustomed social responses, have been dislocated. Even before they set foot on Prospero's island, the members of the court party have begun to lose themselves and their sense of things as they usually are.

The actual wreck of the ship is not staged. Later in the play, in Ariel's narration (I.2.196-215), it appears that certain supernatural phenomena manifested themselves in

7

its final moments. Ferdinand's cry as he threw himself over the side: 'Hell is empty, | And all the devils are here!' expressed every man's thought as fire burst from the masts and rigging. It is important to remember, however, that the storm actually witnessed by the theatre audience contains no hint of the marvellous or extraordinary. Directors who allow Ariel to appear either as flame or in his own person as an actor during the interchanges between the Boatswain, Gonzalo, Antonio, and Sebastian, or introduce Prospero above as a silent but controlling spectator of the action, violate both the text and Shakespeare's general intention. '*Enter Mariners wet*': in this explicit, naturalistic stage direction lies the key to the quality of the scene. For Elizabethans especially, familiar as they were with contemporary accounts of voyages to the New World, *The Tempest* must in its first moments have seemed realistic as the openings of *Twelfth Night* and *As You Like It*, *Cymbeline* or *The Winter's Tale* did not, let alone the spectral encounters of *Hamlet* or *Macbeth*. The characters on stage may be bewildered by the violence of the storm which impels them towards the rocks; the audience in the theatre remains secure in its grasp on the actual until the scene which follows. At this point it too is, without warning, cast adrift.

> *The direful spectacle of the wrack, which touched*
> *The very virtue of compassion in thee,*
> *I have with such provision in mine art*
> *So safely ordered, that there is no soul –*
> *No, not so much perdition as an hair*
> *Betid to any creature in the vessel*
> *Which thou heard'st cry, which thou sawst sink.*

I.2.26–32

Prospero's explanation to Miranda of the illusory nature

of the wreck should come as a complete surprise to the audience. After the matter-of-fact prose of the preceding scene, the realism and the carefully chosen nautical detail, it is a distinct shock to discover that this apparent catastrophe was not what it seemed, was not dangerous at all, but a harmless 'spectacle' stage-managed by an enchanter. It is the first of a number of such surprises which the play has to offer.

In the long second scene the true nature of *The Tempest* begins to declare itself, together with some of its characteristic problems. By contrast with the violence of wind and water just before, the quiet of Prospero's island is, and was meant to seem, uncanny. Equally strange is the dialogue which develops between the magician and his daughter. Placed in the attitude of conversation, these two achieve an oddly limited understanding. Miranda may be aware of her father's art, but this knowledge does not prevent her from viewing the wreck with the eyes of the audience and fearing that the ship and all aboard it have actually perished.

> *Be collected.*
> *No more amazement. Tell your piteous heart*
> *There's no harm done.* I.2.13–15

Prospero's words here reassure both Miranda and the theatre audience. What they significantly do not do is shed any light on the question of how he intends to treat these people once they are assembled on the island. Instead, Prospero plunges into a lengthy and detailed account of those events which deprived him of his dukedom twelve years before. In the course of this account, a relationship which is also a lack of relationship establishes itself between Miranda and himself. As he tries for the first time to tell his daughter who she is and how the two of them came to the island, Prospero becomes emotionally involved with the past in ways that effectively exclude her.

The language of *The Tempest* is in general remarkably compressed, but the tortuous syntax of this narration, its intensity and the anger which contorts many of the phrases, suggest a mind actually re-experiencing pain. Wonder is the basis of Miranda's nature, as of her name, and her occasional interjections are full of astonishment and compassion. What she cannot do, in her innocence and youth, is share or even fully understand her father's feelings. Essentially, she is bewildered by this story which sets out to enlighten her but is continually changing direction as Prospero forgets about or abruptly remembers her presence. To the terrible rhetorical question, 'tell me | If this might be a brother' (I.2.117–18), she replies primly:

> *I should sin*
> *To think but nobly of my grandmother.*
> *Good wombs have borne bad sons.*   I.2.118–20

Prospero has been Miranda's tutor and this is recognizably a sentiment from his own commonplace book (I.2.94–6) slightly altered to fit the occasion. As a response to the dilemma actually posed, however, that of a man's helpless kinship with evil, it is pathetically inadequate. Prospero himself seems aware of the problem. 'Dost thou attend me?' 'Thou attend'st not!' 'I pray thee, mark me.' 'Dost thou hear?' This continual nagging at Miranda in the course of the narration, his anxiety lest she fail to comprehend, emphasizes the distance between father and daughter, the difficulty of communication. And indeed, it will hardly appear subsequently that Miranda has taken in what her father had to tell her. When she first meets Ferdinand, later in this same scene, the prince makes perfectly clear whose son he is. Yet Miranda not only shows no sign of connecting him with the story she has just heard, she seems genuinely perplexed by Prospero's unfriendliness. Never once in her scenes with Ferdinand does she refer to the events of the past or the share which Naples had in them. At the very end of the play, she will be able to bestow an innocent and undifferentiated admiration upon all the courtiers: Alonso, Antonio, and Sebastian, as well as Gonzalo (V.1.181-4).

In another play, such a remarkable lack of concern with the essential facts of a situation might well seem to invite censure. Certainly, Ophelia has been castigated by various commentators on *Hamlet* for behaviour nothing like as obtuse as Miranda's. The fact is, however, that *The Tempest* is not a play that can be reasoned with in terms of character. Even Prospero, its most dominant and fully displayed figure, is curiously opaque. The theatre audience may be privileged to overhear his soliloquies and asides. It watches him in his dealings with a spirit world entirely unavailable to all the other human characters of the play, even Miranda, but it is never really allowed to penetrate his consciousness. Prospero's great speeches, 'Ye elves of hills, brooks, standing lakes, and groves' (V.1.33), or 'Our revels now are ended' (IV.1.148), are strangely externalized utterances. They do not offer what the equivalent speeches of a Hamlet, an Angelo, or a Macbeth offer: an interior landscape, a delineation of the private workings of a mind. In the course of the play, Prospero's words reflect a variety of emotions: irritation, compassion, amusement, bitterness, regret. The feelings themselves are transmitted powerfully by the verse Shakespeare gives him to speak. Their causes, however, at a number of important moments, remain hidden and unexplained. From this distancing of the central character spring many of the problems of the play.

Almost all the action of *The Tempest* is the contrivance of

Prospero. He is at once the inventor and the spectator of the plot, a plot which, as the result of his reticence as a character, is largely mysterious. Once arrived on the island, the members of the court party never know from one moment to another what will happen to them next. Neither, to a very marked extent, does the theatre audience. In the first scene of Act V, at the prompting of Ariel, Prospero asserts that 'The rarer action is | In virtue than in vengeance' (V.1.27–8). He will forgive his enemies and release them from their distraction. But what had he intended to do with them originally? If his thoughts were directed initially towards revenge, towards exacting due punishment for the high wrongs he had suffered, why did he carefully arrange the meeting of Ferdinand and Miranda in Act I? Harsh behaviour to Alonso would hardly be compatible with this marriage. Was he perhaps undecided, still unsure of his own mind when, at the urgent prompting of Fortune, he devised the shipwreck? If so, why is the audience given no hint of this state of indecision? A Prospero explicitly torn between the rival impulses of anger and forgiveness in the early Acts, debating alternative courses of action in soliloquy, would certainly have added to the dramatic tension of a play often criticized for its singular lack of suspense. It is, of course, perfectly possible to speculate about Prospero's intentions in Act I, even as it will be possible to suggest reasons for his behaviour in breaking off the masque so abruptly and with such discomposure in Act IV although, as subsequent events reveal, he had Caliban's conspiracy under perfect control the entire time. Speculations of this kind must, however, remain speculations. The play itself is deliberately enigmatic.

*

In ways that go beyond the problem of Prospero's attitudes,

the impossibility of charting the movement of his mind, *The Tempest* is an extraordinarily secretive work of art. Constantly, it offers the reader or audience half-knowledge where in earlier plays Shakespeare had been delighted to clarify and explain. It invites conjecture. This state of affairs derives in part from a compression, a stripped-down quality, more extreme than anything in Shakespeare's previous work. Linguistically, the play is remarkably intense. Over and over again, the verse achieves an uncanny eloquence by way of what it omits or pares away. So, in Ferdinand's account of Ariel's music, a haunting effect is produced by the suppression of the expected personal pronoun 'I' after two participial phrases which have seemed to lead inevitably towards it:

> *Sitting on a bank,*
> *Weeping again the King my father's wrack,*
> *This music crept by me upon the waters. . . .*
>
> I.2.390–92

Here, and in phrases like the one Prospero uses in his first scene with Miranda, 'the dark backward and abysm of time' (I.2.50), or in Ariel's 'The wild waves whist' (I.2.378), language is subtly dislocated through compression. There is little in the play of that fluent, extended metaphorical writing, the elaborate images generated each from the one before, characteristic of the tragedies or even of *Cymbeline* and *The Winter's Tale*. Instead, *The Tempest* deals in compound words: 'sea-change', 'spell-stopped', 'cloud-capped', 'pole-clipt', 'still-closing', 'hag-seed', 'ever-angry', 'man-monster', 'sight-outrunning', 'sea-sorrow'. In compounds like these – and the play is filled with them – nouns strike against nouns or other parts of speech with an immediacy and force which jars both components out of their accustomed meaning. Sometimes this stark relationship is signalized in the Folio text by a hyphen, sometimes not. The important factor is the brusque juxtaposition of two words neither of which appears to modify or be syntactically dependent upon the other in any normal sense. They have simply been hurled together and left to work out their complex and unstable union within the reader's mind. It is an extreme technique, this yoking together of words deprived quite deliberately of any logical or grammatical link, but it sets up a resonance beyond the capacity of more fully realized, and thereby limited, figures of speech. These paired and evenly weighted words expand almost indefinitely in the consciousness, in widening circles of meaning. Elemental, almost talismanic, images, they seem to be driving towards some ultimate reduction of language, a mode of expression more meaningful in its very bareness than anything a more elaborate and conventional rhetoric could devise. By the end of the play, even single words repeated in isolation – 'sea' or 'wrack' or 'strange' – have acquired the flavour and particularity of metaphor.

The Tempest is an unusually short play by Elizabethan standards, yet it continually gives the impression of being much bigger than it actually is. Like an iceberg, it conceals most of its bulk beneath the surface. The verse gestures repeatedly towards these hidden dimensions, towards a collection of submerged facts about characters and situations which Shakespeare seems to have worked out in his own mind, but which he did not choose to elucidate in the play as it stands. Ferdinand's mysterious reference to Antonio's 'brave son' (I.2.439) as one of the members of the court party cast away in the wreck, a son who neither appears in the play itself nor will ever be mentioned again by anybody, has often been pointed to as evidence of revision, or else of Shakespeare's carelessness in his old age. More probably, Antonio's heir should be seen as part of this shadowy substratum of the drama. He belongs with Sycorax, with Ariel's incarceration in the pine, or with Claribel and that 'sweet marriage' at Tunis which is referred to so often and so ambiguously, but the principals of which we are never to see. In the past, Prospero has dispatched Ariel to fetch dew from 'the still-vexed Bermoothes' (I.2.229) and has performed magical experiments involving the resurrection of the dead (V.1.48–50). Within the play itself, he has a perplexing habit of posing conundrums: 'I | Have given you here a third of mine own life' (IV.1.2–3), or the declaration that once returned to Milan 'Every third thought shall be my grave' (V.1.312). Mathematical precision of this kind positively asks for speculation as to the nature of the other two-thirds. In neither case can an answer be supplied. The dramatist knows, but is not telling.

All the action of *The Tempest* unfolds within a few hours. The play adheres with unusual rigour to the unity of time, and it not only accepts but exploits the consequences of this adherence. A sense of the enormous past bearing upon and almost overwhelming the pin-point of the present is, of course, one of the effects which the unity of time can be used to achieve. Racine does this in *Andromaque*. Aeschylus had employed the technique with sinister effectiveness in the *Agamemnon*. There is something distinctly odd, however, about Shakespeare's back-references in *The Tempest*. Far too many of them never lock into place in the basic present of the drama, never declare their purpose, or even their meaning. The sibylline past of Othello's handkerchief, Katherine's sister who, in *Love's Labour's Lost*, died long ago of her passion, or the recollected merriment of Hamlet's childhood friend Yorick all fit into their respective plays in a perfectly clear-cut and explicable fashion. They are needed in ways that are quite obvious. It is far more difficult to determine the precise function of Claribel in *The Tempest*. In this play, the glimpses provided of a vitally important past, at Milan, on the island, at Tunis, tend to be fragmentary in a way that seems deliberately tantalizing. They are isolated bits of a whole, a few disjointed pieces out of many, which happen to have floated to the surface. There is a great deal more underneath, but its nature and extent can only be guessed at.

All in all, a surprising amount of *The Tempest* depends upon the suppressed and the unspoken. Important scenes are led up to and then not dramatized, like the one in which Prospero makes his peace with Ferdinand and bestows Miranda on him. Between the log-bearing episode at the beginning of Act III and the harmony of the celebration of the betrothal in Act IV, a gap opens. The fact that Prospero's movement of mind from vengeance to mercy, if indeed there is such a movement, cannot be traced causes difficulties enough in the play. There is also his obsessive, and totally unexplained, concern with Miranda's chastity. Exactly what lies behind the melancholy which seems to afflict him in the closing moments? Do his projected meditations upon the subject of the grave represent a purely conventional coming to terms with mortality on the part of a man no longer young? Or do they point to some essential sense of failure, of weariness, haunting a magician whose art has been unable to bring about a true coherence of minds at the end? It would be easier to decide about such important questions if the play itself were less close-mouthed, if Prospero followed the lead of earlier Shakespeare characters and took either the audience or some other character into his confidence.

Other people in the play seem equally baffling. Maddeningly, characters are either given no lines to speak at all, or

else a few, spare words susceptible of a variety of conflict-
ing interpretations, at precisely those moments which cry
out for explanation. So, Ariel announces in the first scene
of Act II that Prospero by his art has foreseen the danger
threatening Alonso and Gonzalo. He wakes the sleepers.
What he significantly declines to tell the audience is
whether or not his master instructed him to exempt
Antonio and Sebastian from the charmed sleep in the first
place. It would be very helpful indeed to be sure that
Prospero deliberately tempted the pair of them, that he
imposed a test, even as it would be useful to know if
Stephano and Trinculo arrived on the island by accident,
or because Prospero saw in them a way of trying Caliban's
nature. These, however, are things which the play will not
divulge. As for the all-important final scene, much of its
quality hangs upon riddles which cannot be resolved: the
tone of voice in which Sebastian should say 'A most high
miracle' (V.1.177) and the precise significance of Antonio's
virtually unbroken silence. It is possible, of course, to
entertain strong personal convictions about passages of
this kind, and to shape the play on the stage accordingly.
It is rarely possible to be sure what is going on inside these
people, or that there is one right way of acting the parts.

The situation is further complicated by the fact that *The
Tempest* is charged with meaning of an essentially non-
verbal kind. Wilson Knight has pointed out that the action
of this play is in itself poetic, that Shakespeare could afford
to strip the verse of extended, formal images precisely
because the whole work is a gigantic metaphor. The plot
in itself has some of the self-sufficient complexity of myth
material. Certainly, it is true that the play stills itself
around a number of stage pictures, visual images out of
which many of the fundamental qualities of the dialogue
seem to grow, but which remain independent of it: the

wreck, the various tableaux of the masque in Act IV, Ariel as a harpy, the shapes which dance about the enchanted banquet, Ferdinand bearing logs, the spirit hounds hunting Caliban and his companions, or Ferdinand and Miranda discovered at chess. More perhaps than with any other work of Shakespeare's, this is a drama which the actors could walk through silently and still manage to convey much of its essential nature. The grouping of characters, the very physical appearance of Ariel and Caliban, of Miranda, or Prospero in his magician's robes, possesses significance. Nor should one forget the omnipresent background of music, the sheer number of songs in the play and the manner in which they draw to themselves and translate emotions which words alone seem inadequate to express.

Even the comic scenes are strikingly independent of language. Quibbles and verbal mistakings, the dazzling and ingenious games that can be played with words, had been the chief resource of Shakespeare's earlier clowns. Launce and Speed, Touchstone, Dogberry, Feste, Lavatch, and the grave-digger in *Hamlet* were all corrupters of words. Stop their mouths and the comedy vanishes. When, on the other hand, Stephano confronts the four-legged monster under the gaberdine in Act II, or misunderstandings spring from the interventions of an invisible Ariel in Act III, *The Tempest* is relying upon immemorial, silent comic patterns, pantomime routines of an essentially non-verbal nature. It is not that Stephano and Trinculo are averse to the pun. They too play with language, but with on the whole a feebleness of invention that betrays how much, for Shakespeare, the life has gone out of this particular kind of verbal exercise. It is difficult to find the ghost of a laugh in those weary explorations of the possible double meanings inherent in 'standard', 'go', and 'line'. It is not for what they say that Stephano and Trinculo are memorable, but for the absurdity, the grotesque humour of the situations in which they involve themselves.

*

Spare, intense, concentrated to the point of being riddling, *The Tempest* provokes imaginative activity on the part of its audience or readers. Its very compression, the fact that it seems to hide as much as it reveals, compels a peculiarly creative response. A need to invent links between words, to expand events and characters in order to understand them, to formulate phrases which can somehow fix the significance of purely visual or musical elements is part of the ordinary experience of reading or watching this play. Sometimes, the process results in a new creation. Certainly it is not by accident that *The Tempest* has generated, or lies at the heart of, so many other works of art. At least two plays of Fletcher's (*The Prophetess* and *The Sea Voyage*, both of 1622) derive from the world of Prospero and his spirits, as do Suckling's *The Goblins* (1638) and Milton's *Comus* (1634). Dryden and Davenant adapted the play, not very happily, to the point of re-creating it. Shelley wrote a verse monologue ('Ariel to Miranda') for one of its characters, Browning ('Caliban Upon Setebos') for another. Mozart sketched out but did not live to write an opera based on it; in Hollywood, a science fiction film (*The Silent Planet*) has actually availed itself of the plot. T. S. Eliot embedded fragments of its verse in *The Waste Land* and, perhaps most brilliantly of all, W. H. Auden has composed an extended meditation, 'The Sea and the Mirror', in which Prospero, Antonio, Caliban, and the rest descant on their own natures and destinies after the end of the play. This is by no means a complete list. Nor does it take into account the independent life, the aura of suggestion, which individual characters, images, or moments of time from the play have acquired in non-fictional writing: social, philosophical, political.

There is a sense in which *The Tempest* is a kind of latter-day myth. Like the story of Oedipus, of Iphigenia, or of Prometheus, the events which occur on Prospero's island possess a meaning at once irreducible and mysterious. They demand interpretation and expansion. The difference, of course, lies in the fact that nothing derived from *The Tempest* is anything like as great or as satisfying as it. It is as though Aeschylus had done what we know he did not: actually invented the story of Agamemnon, Clytemnestra, and the Trojan War and forced all later writers concerned with this material to use the *Oresteia* as their starting-point. Shakespeare's play is virtually unique in that it is a complex and sophisticated work of art, the product of a single mind, which, complete and inviolate in itself, nonetheless is a kind of matrix for further creation. It is easy to mock that bad dramatist F. G. Waldron who, in 1797, tried to assuage the anxiety with which the end of *The Tempest* filled him by composing a sequel to it, a play in which Caliban, Antonio, and Sebastian do indeed betray Prospero on the return voyage to Milan and force him reluctantly to retrieve his book and mend his magic staff. The fact is that, for all its absurdities, *The Virgin Queen* constitutes an entirely proper response to its original. In it, those shadowy figures Sycorax, Claribel, and Claribel's husband actually materialize on the stage. The silence of Antonio is rationalized and explained, and so is Caliban's perfunctory, last-minute change of heart. Prospero becomes an altogether explicable human being, and the universe around him from which he derives his power settles itself into a comfortable, definable pattern. The ending is happy in a way that admits of no doubts. Set

beside *The Tempest* itself, Waldron's creation is ludicrous.
Yet the impulse which produced it is one shared, at least
to some extent, by anyone reading, watching, or producing
the play. Like Auden's 'The Sea and the Mirror', although
it is incomparably less distinguished, *The Virgin Queen*
points to many of the problems and perplexities of *The
Tempest* by way of a departure from and elaboration of
Shakespeare's text.

Criticism of *The Tempest* which regards itself straightforwardly as criticism, rather than derivative creation,
tends to suffer from the fact that it does exactly what
Waldron and Auden do, without acknowledging it. There
has been a persistent tendency to regard the play as allegorical, to feel that the heart of its mystery can be plucked
out by means of some superimposed system of ideas. Whole
books have been written to prove that *The Tempest* is
really an account of the purification and redemption of the
soul as conceived of by Christian mystics, or in the mystery
cults of the pagan world. It has been proclaimed as an
allegory of Shakespeare's own development as an artist,
or of the political situation in Europe at the beginning of
the seventeenth century. Explanations of its peculiarities
have been sought in a supposed dependence upon Neo-
platonism, gnostic thought, the lore of the cabbala, the
Old Testament, or the dramatist's private religious
theories. For some critics, it has made sense only as a
drama of the mind, in which the characters represent
various aspects of Prospero's being in conflict with one
another. At various times the play has been said to be
about almost everything: from the nature of the poetic
imagination to the three-part division of the soul, the
wonders of Renaissance science to man's colonial respon-
sibilities.

Obviously, *The Tempest* cannot be about all these things.

Probably, in fact, it is about none of them. What is remarkable, however, is the degree of superficial plausibility which even the wildest of such theories tends to possess. *The Tempest* is an extraordinarily obliging work of art. It will lend itself to almost any interpretation, any set of meanings imposed upon it: it will even make them shine. The danger of this flexibility, this capacity to illustrate arguments and systems of thought outside itself, is that it can lead critics to mistake what is really their own adaptation for the play. To talk about *The Tempest*, even to try to describe it, without adding to it in terms of motivation, psychology, themes, or ideas, is extremely difficult. As with one of the seminal myths of the classical world, all interpretation beyond a simple outline of the order of events, a list of the people taking part, runs the risk of being incremental. Criticism of this play is often illuminating in itself, as a structure of ideas, without shedding much light on its ostensible subject. It may falsely limit Shakespeare's achievement. Troubling, complex, exasperating, the original is infinitely greater and more suggestive than anything that can be made out of it.

There are, of course, certain definite and objective things which can be said about *The Tempest*. It was, almost without doubt, the last complete play Shakespeare wrote. It occupies pride of place in the Folio of 1623 and the text is extremely good. Stage directions of an unusually elaborate kind are included, although it is difficult to be sure whether these are the work of Shakespeare himself, writing perhaps with an unwonted explicitness because he was no longer in London to instruct the actors personally, or whether they were added from a memory of performance by the scrivener who copied out the text for the printer. The play was performed at Court on Hallowmas night 1611, and again during the winter of 1612–13 as part of the entertainment offered to Princess Elizabeth and her betrothed, the Elector Palatine. It must have been written late in 1610 or, more probably, early in 1611. There is no record of performance at The Globe, but also no reason why Shakespeare's company should not have offered it there. Dryden later claimed that it had been acted with success at Blackfriars playhouse and this seems, on the whole, very likely. *The Tempest* depends heavily upon spectacle and stage machinery, music and atmosphere, of the kind that this theatre was peculiarly well equipped to provide. Finally, in its emphasis upon the sea, upon loss and recovery, travel, chastity, art and nature, parents and children, the play associates itself fairly obviously with that group of romances which also includes *Pericles*, *Cymbeline*, and *The Winter's Tale*.

Aside from this slender body of facts, little is certain. There is evidence that Shakespeare's mind harked back to Montaigne's essay 'On Cannibals' when he came to compose Gonzalo's description of an ideal commonwealth. Prospero's fifth-Act abjuration of magic, 'Ye elves of hills, brooks, standing lakes, and groves', echoes a passage from Ovid's *Metamorphoses*. Apart from these two references, the only source material for *The Tempest* of a definite kind would seem to be the collection of Jacobean pamphlets that deals with the wreck of the *Sea-Adventure* off the coast of Bermuda in 1609. Three of these pamphlets are particularly important: Sylvester Jourdain's *Discovery of the Bermudas* (1610), the Council of Virginia's *True Declaration of the state of the Colony in Virginia* (1610), and William Strachey's *True Reportory of the Wrack*. This last work, although it was written like the others in 1610, was not actually published until 1625, when it appeared as part of *Purchas His Pilgrimes*. Shakespeare must, therefore, have had enough interest in the subject to read it in manuscript. From all three of these accounts, Strachey's in particular, *The Tempest* collected suggestions and details. A storm at sea made more terrifying by flashes of St Elmo's fire, mutiny and insurrection on the island, the unfamiliar wildlife of the New World, the unexpected rescue when all seemed lost: in the experiences of the Virginia colonists whose journey was so rudely but, as it turned out, fortunately interrupted, Shakespeare may well have found the impulse for his play.

The Bermuda pamphlets did not provide him, however, with either his characters or, except in the most generalized sense, his plot. Exactly where they came from is, and seems likely to remain, a mystery. Persistent attempts have been made to establish a connexion between *The Tempest* and a German play written before 1605 by Jacob Ayrer, *Die Schöne Sidea*. Various Spanish romances, the story of Prospero Adorno, Duke of Genoa, as related in Thomas's *History of Italy* (1549), Virgil's *Aeneid*, and some of the skeleton plots of the *Commedia dell'arte* have also been proposed, together with a number of folk tales. In general, it seems improbable that Shakespeare depended, in devising his characters and story, upon anything other than a quite unlocalized consciousness of certain motifs and story patterns widely distributed through the literature of the world. Enchanted islands, magicians with beautiful daughters, deceptive banquets, swords which freeze in their bearers' grasp, or the task imposed upon the prince who would win the mysterious lady, all constitute quite familiar elements in a variety of literatures. There is no reason to suppose that Shakespeare was drawing upon anything more specific than a widespread and fundamentally oral tradition. There is little that is complicated, in the sense of intrigue or interwoven story lines, about the plot of *The Tempest*. It is simple, monolithic, and unadorned. Nothing about it suggests that Shakespeare was building upon another, individual, work of art, the discovery of which could illuminate his own achievement.

*

More promising, perhaps, than any attempt to explain *The Tempest* by way of its sources is the question of its adherence to the classical unities of time, place, and action. This is a straightforward fact about the play, and one of enormous importance. Here, for some reason, Shakespeare chose to contradict the practice of a lifetime and construct a drama according to neo-classical principles. The setting throughout (leaving aside the introductory first scene) is Prospero's island; the time which elapses is roughly four hours; the parts of the action are bound together tightly into a whole. The play makes an obeisance to the authority of the ancient world, as Elizabethans conceived of it, particularly striking by contrast with the licence of *Cymbeline* and *The Winter's Tale* just before. Shakespeare had, of course, taking over the structure of his Plautine original, submitted himself to the unities years before in *The Comedy of Errors*. In *The Tempest*, on the other hand, concentration of this kind was not native to the material with which he was working. Moreover, the effect produced is odd as it was not in the earlier play. The unities themselves were, after all, for Elizabethans servants of what Italian Renaissance critics liked to call *verisimile*. It was considered absurd to ask an audience to regard the same stage as representing more than one place, to countenance the passing of more than twenty-four hours within the time of the performance, to accept multiple lines of action: absurd in the sense of being psychologically impossible, violating that lifelikeness, that truth to nature, which drama must maintain in order to convince. The paradoxical fact about the use of the unities in *The Tempest*, however, is that they in no way serve the interests of *verisimile*. Quite the opposite: they make a strange tale even stranger. Like hounds, the strictures of Aristotle crouch for employment before Prospero's magic, and are dispatched on unfamiliar errands.

On two important occasions in *The Tempest*, Prospero inquires the time from Ariel. In the first instance, in Act I, his question serves to indicate how long he expects the action to take: 'The time 'twixt six and now | Must by us both be spent most preciously' (I.2.240–41). The second, at the beginning of Act V, assures the audience that he is indeed accomplishing his purposes within the span of time allotted for them (V.1.4–5). Alonso in the final scene goes out of his way to point out that Ferdinand cannot have known Miranda for even three hours, and the Boatswain shortly thereafter measures the space between the wreck and the re-discovery of his ship by the passage of 'three glasses' (V.1.223). These persistent references only emphasize the fact that the amount of action unfolded is too great for the time-span in which it is contained. The storm, the birth and destruction of the plots of Antonio and Sebastian, Caliban and Stephano, the testing of Ferdinand, the winning of Miranda and regeneration of Alonso, cannot be huddled together within the space of four hours without contributing to the unreality of the play, rather than its truth to nature. Continual reference to Prospero's magic becomes necessary in the way of explanation. Only in dreams does life move with such bewildering and irrational speed: in dreams, or else in the dreamlike world ruled by an enchanter.

Like the unity of time, the unity of place is essentially magical. All the characters of the play, human, half-human, and spirit, are assembled on the island, combined into little groups or violently separated from one another in an entirely arbitrary fashion, according to the dictates of Prospero's will. They cannot leave this place without his permission, cannot even control the direction in which their footsteps stray. His magic also controls the unity of action. What happens in *The Tempest*, from the shipwreck with which it begins to the reconciliation at the end, is his work. He is like a dramatist contriving a play, except that he exists himself within the illusion he spins. Shakespeare had once before given a character a position of this kind: the Duke in *Measure for Measure*. Not only did the Duke, however, lack the power and control of Prospero, but the material upon which he worked set up resistance suggesting the fundamental opposition between life and art, the reluctance of reality to accommodate itself to the formal patterns of drama. In Vienna, the Duke was surrounded with characters who defied his arrangements for them, and whose unpredictable wills were continually upsetting the plot: Lucio and Barnardine, Juliet, Angelo, Isabella, and Mariana. With Prospero, and his possession of a magic so powerful that it could control the god worshipped by Sycorax, there is never any such feeling. Only at one point in the play is there any suggestion of events escaping his control, and there the insurrection is quelled by Ariel with such negligent ease that generations of commentators have wondered why Prospero should break off the performance of the masque with such indications of anxiety and distress.

Yet despite the sureness of his handling of the plot, Prospero too has his limitations, limitations which are important in the scheme of the play as a whole. In his own sphere, he may be absolute master of action. His sway seems to be confined, however, to the island itself and not effective beyond it. Not until the reign of 'A most auspicious star' (I.2.182) did his enemies come within his reach, a moment for which Fortune has made him wait twelve years. His art confers on him some of the power of the gods. He can raise the winds and darken the sun, shake the earth and command spirits unsubdued by the black magic of a witch like Sycorax. He can even raise the dead. What his white magic cannot do is, significantly, the one thing that matters most: to alter the nature and inclinations of the individual human heart. The souls of Ferdinand and Gonzalo, Antonio and Caliban, remain, for good or ill, their own. Prospero can freeze Ferdinand in his tracks, can charm his nerves and sword, but he cannot make him fall in love with Miranda. All he can do is bring the two together and hope that from this carefully arranged meeting love will spring. His wishes are fulfilled: 'At the first sight | They have changed eyes' (I.2.441–2), but even so doubt remains. Only by imposing a period of trial upon Ferdinand and, in a slightly different sense, upon Miranda as well can Prospero feel sure that this love is deeply grounded. And even then, he is tormented by fears that Ferdinand's sexual desire will overmaster his honour, and that Miranda will yield.

With the sinners of the play, Prospero's effectiveness is even more limited. Caliban serves him perforce, under the threat of cramps, side-stitches, the stings of adders, and the pinches of malicious goblins. He remains, however, despite this formidable physical intimidation, and despite the attempts at education and humanization lavished on him in the past:

> *A devil, a born devil, on whose nature*
> *Nurture can never stick; on whom my pains,*
> *Humanely taken, all, all lost, quite lost.*
> *And as with age his body uglier grows,*
> *So his mind cankers.*   IV.1.188–92

28

It is true that, at the very end of the play, Caliban determines to be 'wise hereafter, | And seek for grace' (V.1.295–6). Essentially, though, the remark seems to reflect a primitive recognition that Stephano was in no sense a plausible substitute as master for Prospero, particularly for a Prospero made more impressive by his ducal finery. It does not take Caliban very far in the direction of those values of reason, chastity, and self-control which Prospero had long ago tried to instil in him. At the end of the play as at its beginning he is a 'thing of darkness' still (V.1.275).

Alonso, Antonio, and Sebastian also measure the extent of Prospero's power. Through spells and deceiving shows he drives the three men of sin into a distraction. Their senses become his prisoners, their bodies helpless and immobilized. But once they are released from this enchantment there can be no assurance of penitence, of any change of heart. Such a transformation is beyond the power of what Prospero disparagingly terms his 'rough magic' (V.1.50) to exact. It is the point at which his art stops short. Here, his command is less than that of Shakespeare himself, who could at will change the jealousy of Orlando's brother Oliver into remorse in *As You Like It*, the contempt of Bertram in *All's Well that Ends Well* into love. As things turn out, Prospero will be able to count Alonso as one of his successes. The King of Naples is moved to his innermost being by what has happened to him on the island, utterly sincere in his prayer for forgiveness. This result, however, is more or less an accident, not something enforced by magic art. It is perhaps a bitter consciousness of incapacity, a premonition of failure, which suddenly oppresses Prospero in Act IV, while the Nymphs and Reapers are moving through their formal measures. In itself, Caliban's plot is not dangerous. But its very existence serves to remind Prospero that with the members of the court party as with Caliban all his work may come to nothing. The text at this point is so reticent as to make critical certainty impossible, but it is at least arguable that some such link between the failure with Caliban and the potential failure with Alonso, Antonio, and Sebastian is responsible for the poisoning of Prospero's joy in the betrothal. He is not vulnerable, despite Caliban's hopes, to a clumsy physical assault by two fools and a man-monster armed with stakes and knives. It is Caliban's unalterable will to evil and what it may forbode to Prospero's other human experiments which destroys his peace.

*

The Tempest is a remarkably compartmentalized play. That Prospero himself should be a lonely and isolated figure is, in a sense, the product of his role as dramatist. His contact with a world of spirits invisible to everyone else also serves to cut him off from the other human characters of the play. Yet it is hard not to feel that Shakespeare has deliberately pushed the solitude of his central character to an extreme. Prospero's daughter is the dearest thing he has, 'a third of mine own life, | Or that for which I live' (IV.1.3–4), but there is a surprising lack of genuine communication between them throughout the play, nor does he ever take her into his confidence. Ironically, her union with Ferdinand, so earnestly desired by Prospero, only serves to increase this distance between father and daughter. When Prospero pretends to quarrel with the prince and sets him to work bearing logs, Miranda's heart is torn between an old loyalty and a new. She has been instructed *not* to plead for Ferdinand, to remai n aloo from him, and not to tell him her name. She disobeys in every particular. That she should do so without hesitation is right and a measure of the depth of her passion. It involves nonetheless a transfer of basic allegiance from her father to her lover. This is a necessary prologue to the marriage Prospero plans for the couple, but it leaves him even more alone. There is a strange wistfulness about his interchanges with Ariel in the latter part of the play, the endearments which replace the brusque commands of the early Acts, the note of affectionate regret at parting with him forever, as though this frail relationship with a spirit, a thing of air, had become a substitute for more ordinary contacts.

The other characters of *The Tempest* are divided sharply into groups. The spirit world, that of Ariel and his minions, is set apart automatically from the human. Beyond it, Ferdinand and Miranda comprise one unit, the triumvirate of Caliban, Trinculo, and Stephano a second, and the members of the court party a third. There is, moreover, the suggestion of still another division within this last unit, setting Antonio and Sebastian apart from their companions. The Boatswain and sailors exist at a fourth remove. Prospero may possess knowledge of all these groups, and power over them; they themselves are woefully ignorant of one another's existence for most of the play. Not until the final scene do the members of the court party encounter Prospero and Miranda, or realize that Ferdinand is not drowned. At the same late moment Ferdinand himself discovers that his father and the courtiers have reached the island, and Miranda first sets eyes on the creatures who will inhabit her brave new world. The Boatswain learns that his passengers are safe as well as his ship. The three participants in the comic action astonish everyone but Prospero by making a public appearance and are astonished themselves to learn how populous the island is, after their conviction that it harboured five people only, including themselves.

The Tempest may observe the unity of action, but it does so in a curiously abstract, almost undramatic sense. It is impossible to detach the love of Ferdinand and Miranda, the conspiracy of Antonio and Sebastian, or the ambitions of Stephano, from the mainstream of Prospero's purpose. All the parts of this play are welded together; there are no separate, independent actions. Yet the relationship between groups is not based upon meetings and dialogue, as in most plays. The majority of the characters set sail originally in the same ship, bound for Naples. Once dispersed upon the island, however, their association depends firstly upon the fact that all of them meet in the consciousness of Prospero, if nowhere else, and secondarily upon certain thematic parallels which become clear to the theatre audience as the play proceeds. It was exceptionally silly of Dryden in his adaptation, *The Enchanted Island* (1667), to endow both Miranda and Caliban with sisters, Ariel with a fiancée, and to balance Miranda's inexperience with that of Hippolito, a man who has never seen a woman. Nevertheless, as with so many elaborations and expansions of *The Tempest*, this one constitutes a response to something fundamental and puzzling in the original. Doublings of character and action, parallels which sometimes point up similarity but more often contrast, are among the basic organizing principles of the play. So, Ariel and Caliban are obviously conceived of as antithetical, both in nature and appearance. Caliban's sullen wood-bearing contrasts with Ferdinand's gracious accomplishment of the same task; his failure to profit by education with Miranda's malleability. Two conspiracies against a sleeping victim are launched in the play: one by Antonio, the other by Caliban. They ask to be compared and, in the comparison, a parallel develops between the natural and the sophisticated savage which is scarcely to the advantage of Prospero's brother. Prospero's white magic is the opposite of the black art practised by Sycorax. There are a great many more of these connexions. When Dryden, in 1667, extended them he produced a work that was both sensational and crude. Behind it, however, lay a genuine feeling for how *The Tempest* works.

Even within distinct groups of characters, communication is oddly imperfect. Prospero and Miranda, from the very first scene of the play onwards, seem to talk across an abyss. With Ferdinand she does achieve an intense, essentially non-verbal rapport, but the first stages of their conversation are perplexed in the extreme. Antonio and Sebastian also, after some initial misunderstandings, reach a communion. 'Do you not hear me speak?' 'thou speak'st | Out of thy sleep. What is it thou didst say?' 'What stuff is this? | How say you?' 'Do you understand me?' – these nagging questions passing back and forth between the two conspirators in the first scene of Act II are strongly reminiscent of Prospero's need to be reassured in the preceding Act that what he said was being understood by Miranda. In the case of Antonio and Sebastian, the inquiries come from both sides, not simply one. At the end of the interchange they have attained a communion of evil, an entire understanding, which asks to be set up beside the communion of innocence and trust arrived at by Ferdinand and Miranda. These are the only examples of a true meeting of minds in the play and it is a little frightening to reflect that, by their opposed nature, they come close to cancelling each other out.

In part, the difficulty which people experience in understanding one another springs from the abnormality of their mental condition. *The Tempest* is very much a drama of strange states of consciousness. Characters fall helplessly into enchanted sleeps, as Miranda does in Act I, or most of the members of the court party in Act II. Ferdinand's mind, even before he makes his first appearance, has already been affected in ways he himself does not understand by the power of Ariel's music. His father's supposed death, from which he is separated by no more than a few minutes, grows small in the distance. He is able to turn at once to Miranda, to mistake her for a goddess, and to yield to Prospero with the admission that his spirits, 'as in a dream, are all bound up' (I.2.487). Subsequently, he will be isolated with Miranda in a lovers' realm of private, essentially uncommunicable, experience. Alonso enters the play locked up in a lonely, intensely personal, world of grief. Although his courtiers continually address him, either to comfort or to accuse, he is only minimally aware of their presence. His consciousness is barred and shuttered against their words. For Caliban and his two companions, existence is artificially heightened during most of the play by inebriation. Even the Master and the Boatswain make their final appearance in Act V 'in a dream' (V.1.239). The three men of sin, Alonso, Sebastian, and Antonio, are driven into a frenzy at the end of the banquet scene in Act III. Gonzalo and the rest mourn over this distraction without really being able to comprehend it. When Prospero undoes the spell at the beginning of Act V, his victims have wandered so far, mentally, from normal modes of apprehension that he finds himself delivering his first speech of mingled welcome and reproach to the empty air: 'Not one of them | That yet looks on me, or would know me' (V.1.82–3). Three times in the play (I.2.176, IV.1.163, V.1.246) a character describes his own or someone else's mind as 'beating' against the situation enmeshing it. This sense of the blood-pulse drumming through and obscuring the supposedly rational processes is central to *The Tempest*, part of the reason why people find understanding so difficult.

Further problems arise from the fact that experience in the play is curiously relative. The thunderstorm which Caliban, Trinculo, and Stephano encounter in the second scene of Act II appears not to exist for anyone else. Alonso, Antonio, and Sebastian hear the accusation levelled against them by the harpy in the banquet scene; Gonzalo and the others do not and are at a loss to explain their companions' wild words and 'strange stare' (III.3.96). The island itself seems to change character bewilderingly according to the nature of the person regarding it. For the back-biters and sinners, Prospero's domain seems dry and barren. The ground is tawny, the air pestilent, 'as 'twere perfumed by a fen' (II.1.51). Adrian and Gonzalo, on the other hand, standing in exactly the same place, looking at the same prospect, can talk only of the sweetness of the breeze and the green luxuriance of the grass. A similar discrepancy declares itself over the question of their garments, drenched in the sea. When Gonzalo remarks upon their uncanny brilliance, 'being rather new-dyed than stained with salt water' (II.1.66–7), he is met by the incredulity of the wicked, for whom the miracle simply does not exist. Even Caliban, untrustworthy though he is, administers a slight shock to the audience when he suddenly presents his own view of the wrong done him by Prospero in usurping the island. Caliban is by no means the downtrodden hero of the play, but his account of how his original love for his master turned to hate has a certain validity (I.2.331–44). He has omitted one salient fact, his attempt while still in a position of trust to violate Miranda. All the same, this picture of the past as seen through his eyes must be set beside Prospero's. Again, it serves to stress the fact that there are almost as many opposed ways of seeing a given event or moment of time as there are characters involved.

＊

In the long final scene of *The Tempest*, a scene comprising in fact the entire fifth Act, there seems at last to be hope that the compartments of the play, its relativity of vision, will be broken down. Here, all the human characters come together for the first time. The spirit world, it is true, remains aloof. An Ariel invisible to everyone else on the stage continues to communicate with Prospero, and Prospero alone. All the others, however, are present and disenchanted. Sore and limping, Caliban and his companions have been tormented into a state of entire sobriety. The spell which bound up the senses of Alonso, Sebastian, and Antonio is undone:

> *Their understanding*
> *Begins to swell, and the approaching tide*
> *Will shortly fill the reasonable shore*
> *That now lies foul and muddy.*   V.i.79–82

Gonzalo recognizes that, improbable though it seems, what confronts him now is certain fact, not one of the deceiving subtleties of the isle. Ferdinand and Miranda are revealed at chess. Even the Master and the Boatswain put in their appearance, in order to make the cast of characters complete. It is *The Tempest*'s version of that moment characteristic of all romances in which the lost are restored, the wrongs of the past forgiven, in which misunderstandings are unravelled and characters speak and feel as one. Structurally, what Shakespeare is doing here is perfectly familiar; his actual handling of the scene, however, is highly unorthodox.

Gonzalo speaks what in another play would have been the valediction:

> *Was Milan thrust from Milan that his issue*
> *Should become kings of Naples? O, rejoice*

Beyond a common joy, and set it down
With gold on lasting pillars. In one voyage
Did Claribel her husband find at Tunis,
And Ferdinand her brother found a wife
Where he himself was lost; Prospero his dukedom
In a poor isle, and all of us ourselves
When no man was his own.   V.1.205-13

It is tempting to be caught by the sheer beauty of this formulation of the *felix culpa*, to isolate it from its dramatic context and so make it seem more important than it is. The truth is that what Gonzalo says does not sum up the play now reaching its end. His speech would by no means be subscribed to, in fact, by most of the other characters. Miranda and even Ferdinand are too innocent to understand. Caliban, Stephano, and Trinculo understand even less. Even if they possessed more knowledge than they do about the events of the past four hours, what Gonzalo is trying to say would remain irrelevant to them. As for Antonio and Sebastian, frustrated and unregenerate, they do not seem to rejoice at all, let alone in the measure proposed. It is hard to feel that they come any closer here to seeing what Gonzalo sees than they had come in Act II, when they greeted his claim that the island was green and temperate, and their clothes fresh, with derision.

Prospero himself, the man responsible for everything, still stands apart. His attitude weary and obscurely tinged with gloom, he is divided from the others by a barrier more fundamental than that of the magic art he has now relinquished. To Miranda's impulsive judgement, 'O brave new world, | That has such people in't', he can only rejoin, ''Tis new to thee' (V.1.183-4). He stands at the last with his successes beside him, in the form of Alonso, Ferdinand, and Miranda. Gonzalo's native

37

goodness has survived the years unimpaired. Yet Prospero is not really of their kind. Even worse, he must share the stage with his failures: Caliban, the 'thing of darkness' (V.1.275) for whom he must acknowledge responsibility, and Antonio and Sebastian, who cannot be wished away either. There is something disturbing about Prospero's speech of forgiveness to his brother:

> For you, most wicked sir, whom to call brother
> Would even infect my mouth, I do forgive
> Thy rankest fault – all of them; and require
> My dukedom of thee, which perforce, I know,
> Thou must restore.   V.1.130–34

It is scarcely the pardon of a Christian, or a truly forgiving man. Contempt breathes through it, a basic inability to forget and put aside, not genuine mercy. Comedies do not usually end in this spirit. Equally disturbing is the fact that Alonso is never, apparently, to know about his own brother's attempt to kill him. 'At this time', Prospero remarks quietly to the two of them, 'I will tell no tales' (V.1.128–9). It is recognizably a silence dependent upon their future good behaviour, but it runs counter to the conventions of comedy. Oliver, too, in *As You Like It*, tried to murder his brother. At the end of the play, this fact is not only out in the open, Oliver has repented and been restored to trust. Sebastian, on the other hand, has nothing to say to Prospero's private revelation, except 'The devil speaks in him' (V.1.129), a remark which by no stretch of the imagination could be conceived of as an expression of penitence.

Apart from Sebastian's ambiguous exclamation in the instant that Ferdinand and Miranda are discovered, the wicked lords speak only once again in the play. When

Caliban, Stephano, and Trinculo are driven in by Ariel, they momentarily find their tongues:

SEBASTIAN   *Ha, ha!*
  What things are these, my lord Antonio?
  Will money buy 'em?
ANTONIO   *Very like. One of them*
  Is a plain fish, and no doubt marketable.   V.1.263–6

The derisory manner, the sneering utterance which, as Coleridge once remarked, Shakespeare never makes habitual with any but bad men, is still with them. Sebastian comments twice more upon Stephano, and asks him a question, after which the two lords sink back into silence. About the reunion between Alonso and his son, the reconciliation of Naples and Milan, the betrothal of the young lovers, they have had no word to say. Only the opportunity for expressing contempt with safety can draw them into speech. Standing, obviously, side by side and a little apart from the others, they are at one in their silence as in their brief flicker of conversation. They refuse to be absorbed into any final harmony. Neither can they be conveniently got rid of.

The dramatist Waldron may have gone to extremes when he interpreted this fifth-Act behaviour of Antonio and Sebastian as the prelude to another conspiracy, one which would cause Prospero some extremely bad moments on the return voyage. It is significant, however, that even Dryden, despite the fact that he had omitted the character Sebastian and the whole plot against Alonso in his version of the play, felt impelled to provide Antonio with a full and convincing declaration of repentance. He also left Prospero still secure in the possession of his magic power at the end – just in case. The presence of this 'brace of lords' (V.1.126) is profoundly disquieting in Shakespeare's final scene. Their silence comes, gradually, to press upon the happiness of the others like an increasing and ominous weight. They are the unfinished business of the play, loose ends which are not and indeed cannot be tied up. Comedy villains are normally dealt with in one of two ways at the conclusion of the action. Their plots foiled, they either repent like Orlando's brother and are rewarded by being accepted as redeemed members of the comic society or, like Don John in *Much Ado About Nothing*, they remain unregenerate. In the latter case, they must expect to be punished and violently cast out. Dryden chose to regularize *The Tempest* in accordance with the first alternative when he made Antonio genuinely contrite. Waldron chose the second when he left Antonio and Sebastian, their conspiracy finally overthrown, confined for ever on the island while the others sailed home merrily to Naples. Again, the changes introduced by men concerned to re-create Shakespeare's work in their own terms point to something odd in the original.

Even at its ending, *The Tempest* remains compartmentalized. Distinct groups of characters meet at last, but they do not really communicate with one another, and the magician who has ordered these revelations and discoveries is still essentially alone. As in the paintings of Piero della Francesca, the eyes even of people confronting one another directly in conversation do not seem to meet. Instead, the lines of sight stray off at angles. There is a puzzling obliquity of vision. The coming together of all the characters at the end, a meeting so long expected, only serves to stress the essential lack of relationship, in ways that have an overtone of tragedy. It is true that Prospero promises to explain later. He will tell the courtiers, beyond the limits of the play,

the story of my life,
And the particular accidents gone by
Since I came to this isle.   V.1.305-7

From this recital, presumably, they will gain some understanding of their own fortunes since the wreck. In the
actual time of the play, however, only a very few people
come to any realization of the nature and extent of Prospero's power, or the fact that their strange adventures
were of his making. The degrees of their knowledge are
as various as the kinds of characters, but all are incomplete.

With characteristic piety, but also with a certain obtuse-
ness, Gonzalo ascribes the happy outcome to heaven.

I have inly wept,
Or should have spoke ere this. Look down, you gods,
And on this couple drop a blessèd crown!
For it is you that have chalked forth the way
Which brought us hither.   V.1.200-204

This is all very well. Gonzalo, however, knows nothing
about Ariel and his minions, nothing about Prospero's
guiding hand on the action during the last four hours. His
confident ascription of what has proved to be a fortunate
outcome to the benevolence of heaven seems to the
better-informed theatre audience a hasty and ill-formed
judgement. Aside from the ambiguous part played by
Providence and an auspicious star in bringing Miranda
and her father safely to the island in the first place, and,
later, in leading Prospero's enemies within striking distance, the role of the gods in this play is indefinite in the
extreme. Reference, at this point, to *King Lear* seems
relevant. Edgar, in that play, takes upon himself what
is really the task of the gods when he contrives his blind

father's mock suicide and subsequent restoration. He bids Gloucester

> *Think that the clearest gods, who make them honours*
> *Of men's impossibilities, have preserved thee.*
>
> King Lear, IV.6.72–3

Gloucester believes these words. His faith in a heaven which directs human destinies, however erratically and mysteriously, is restored. The theatre audience, on the other hand, has just seen Edgar carefully arrange his father's fall. It cannot accept an explanation of this kind. What it is confronted with instead is a man who, in desperation, has assumed the role of the gods in another man's life. There is an immense grandeur in the fact that a human being can shoulder divine responsibility of this kind in the callous and unexplained absence of the proper powers. Such an attempt cannot, however, by its very nature, be entirely successful. About Lear and Cordelia's defeat in battle, Edgar can do nothing. Eventually, he has to explain himself and his actions to his father. When he does so, Gloucester dies.

Like Edgar, Prospero has, with the help of his magic art, played the part of heaven. His sphere of influence has been far wider, the number of people caught up in his net much greater, his power considerably more impressive. In a play which presents Caliban as an image of man at his owest, half-merged with the animal, Prospero stands at the other extreme of that free ascent which Pico della Mirandola imagined in his fifteenth-century oration 'On the Dignity of Man'. Man alone, the Creator tells Adam, has no definite place assigned him in the universe between the beasts and the angels.

Neither a fixed abode nor a form that is thine alone nor any function peculiar to thyself have We given thee, Adam, to the end that according to thy longing and according to thy judgement thou mayst have and possess what abode, what form, and what functions thou thyself shalt desire. The nature of all other beings is limited and constrained within the bounds of laws prescribed by Us. Thou, constrained by no limits, in accordance with thine own free will, in whose hand We have placed thee, shalt ordain for thyself the limits of thy nature. We have set thee at the world's centre that thou mayst from thence more easily observe whatever is in the world. We have made thee neither of heaven nor of earth, neither mortal nor immortal, so that with freedom of choice and with honour, as though the maker and moulder of thyself, thou mayst fashion thyself in whatever shape thou shalt prefer. Thou shalt have the power to degenerate into the lower forms of life, which are brutish. Thou shalt have the power, out of thy soul's judgement, to be reborn into the higher forms, which are divine.

As the maker and moulder of himself, Prospero has indeed overcome the limitations confining more ordinary humans. Through his own efforts he has come to partake, at least to some extent, of the divine. When Ariel, addressing the three men of sin in the banquet scene, describes himself and his cohorts as the 'ministers of Fate' (III.3.62) and tells Alonso, Antonio, and Sebastian that they are now in the hands and at the mercy of the outraged powers of heaven, he is not, strictly speaking, telling the truth. The members of the court party are in the personal control of Prospero, a Prospero who has in fact written this very speech for Ariel to deliver. Yet there is a sense in which Prospero stands, through much of the play, as a successful

43

substitute for heaven. As a judge of good and evil, handing out reward for the one and punishment for the other, he is accurate and scrupulously fair. This is the way the gods should act. The trouble is that, as it was for Edgar, Prospero's success is in the end incomplete. His is a rough magic after all, incapable of affecting the human heart. It isolates the mage from his own kind without really assimilating him to the realm of the higher spirits. In the end, he must give it up, must accept his own humanity and its most painful and inevitable consequence: the fact of death.

*

The Tempest begins by deliberately mystifying its audience. After the realism of the opening storm at sea, the scene between Prospero and Miranda which follows is meant to surprise, to indicate that this is a drama in which it is rash to believe things apparently certain. In the play as a whole, the equilibrium of the spectators is continually being upset. As the contriver of action, Prospero relies heavily upon theatrical elements, little plays within the play of *The Tempest*. He uses these performances sometimes to terrify, sometimes to delight. Always, however, they are ambiguous, leaving the theatre audience as well as the characters on stage in a state of confusion. In Shakespeare's earlier work, the play-within-the-play had served a variety of purposes. Up to the point of *Pericles*, however, the distinction set up between different levels of reality had remained essentially clear. With the Mouse-trap play in *Hamlet*, the Pyramus and Thisbe interlude in *A Midsummer Night's Dream*, or the impersonations undertaken by Falstaff and Prince Hal in the Boar's Head Tavern scene of *1 Henry IV*, there was never any doubt concerning the division between illusory world and real world, the actor and the ordinary man. It was possible and in fact exciting to play with the line of demarcation, but always in the consciousness that reality must triumph in the end. Not until the last plays did Shakespeare begin to obliterate this former distinction, to break down the barrier separating audience and actors. *The Tempest* represents the extreme stage of this development, the extension of that meditation upon the nature of the theatre itself already so marked in *Cymbeline* and *The Winter's Tale*.

In Prospero's hands, the play-within-the-play becomes an agent of bewilderment. It is a means of complicating still further an already baffling island, full of noises and strange apparitions, where sleep and waking are states oddly hard to tell apart, and nothing stays the same from one moment to the next. The members of the court party are already weary and perplexed at the beginning of the third scene of Act III. All sorts of things have happened to them which they do not understand: the odd nature of the wreck, the fresh colours which their garments have borrowed from the sea, the unexplained sleep of Act II, mysterious sounds, a humming in the ears. Even the paths which they follow in their despairing search for Ferdinand seem designed to perplex. 'Here's a maze trod indeed', Gonzalo sighs, as though this journey led them through the artificial labyrinth of some great, formal garden, not across a wild and supposedly uninhabited island (III.3.2–3). At this point, they are confronted with what Sebastian calls 'A living drollery' (III.3.22) in the form of those strange shapes who enter with a banquet, dance about it, and then vanish. Not only Sebastian, but also Antonio, Alonso, and Gonzalo regard this spectacle as proof that no fiction, no fabulous story, can now be doubted. The phoenix, the unicorn, monstrous men dewlapped like bulls: all of these virtual synonyms for the

45

incredible and the illusory acquire a substantial life in the eyes of the courtiers as the result of what they have just seen. Their ordinary criteria of belief, their day-to-day sense of the distinctions to be drawn between things illusory and things real, have been shattered.

The theatre audience, of course, is more advantageously placed than the nobles. It is aware of Prospero stage-managing the spectacle from above, invisible to his victims. It can hear his asides; it watches him direct his spirits, and is party to his final commendation of the actors, Ariel and his fellows. For Alonso, Gonzalo, and their companions, the banquet is an unexplained wonder. For the audience, it is a masque. Indeed, stripped of its accusatory finale, the banquet scene of *The Tempest* might almost be one of those elaborately impromptu tableaux designed to surprise James I as he strolled through the greenery of some great nobleman's park. Sixteenth- and seventeenth-century monarchs were continually being startled and (it was hoped) pleased by being swept into a little dramatic performance masquerading as reality. So, in the year 1578, Queen Elizabeth walking, as the account says,

> *in Wanstead Garden, as she passed down into the grove, there came suddenly, among the train, one apparelled like an honest man's wife of the country, where crying out for justice, and desiring all the lords and gentlemen to speak a good word for her, she was brought to the presence of her majesty, to whom upon her knees she offered a supplication, and used this speech.*

This is the beginning of Sir Philip Sidney's masque *The Lady of May*, with its debate between the rival claims of the shepherd and the forester, a debate which Elizabeth herself was asked to resolve at the end. Prospero's enchanted banquet, the dance of monsters, and the sudden intrusion of the harpy are generically things which royalty might perfectly well have met with in the course of an afternoon's walk.

For Alonso and the others, however, coming upon it on a deserted island in the midst of the sea, Prospero's show cannot be seen as part of any princely welcome. For them, it is masque material metamorphosed into reality: a *living* drollery, and a matter for astonishment and some fear. The theatre audience is wiser than this. Yet there is a sense in which it too is unsure, is fooled with art. There has been no preparation for this little play-scene, no explanation of Prospero's purposes. The accusation at the end comes as a surprise. Also, the nature of the actors is strange in a way that effectively upsets convention. Normally, the actor is a person with a real and single identity who, in the exercise of his profession, assumes a whole series of illusory *personae*. He is nearer to the world of the theatre audience as Sir Laurence Olivier than as Sir Laurence Olivier temporarily representing the character of Othello. This is not true, however, of Prospero's minions. These disembodied spirits have shape and form only when they are acting. Take away their assumed roles, their disguises, and they become less instead of more real by ordinary standards. They simply vanish into air, into thin air. Even with Ariel, it is hard to distinguish his true identity behind the multitude of disguises in which he manifests himself: as the fiery phenomenon of the storm, the nymph of the sea, the harpy, the goddess Ceres, the disembodied voice. Air is his element; he becomes palpable only as a concession to human power. The superior knowledge possessed by the theatre audience does not pluck out the heart of the mystery of Prospero's masque. It merely leads into an appearance–reality dilemma more profound and more complex than the one perceived by characters actually on the stage.

These quicksands, this meddling with the ordinary relationships of the theatre, become even more obvious in the second of the major plays-within-the-play: the masque which Prospero presents for the delectation of Ferdinand and Miranda in Act IV. This time, the stage audience is aware that it is a theatrical performance it watches. Ferdinand and Miranda are not susceptible to the mistakes of the court party. For a while, it seems as though there were an orderly recession here of three planes of reality: the theatre audience, the audience on the stage, and, finally, the actors in the masque. It is true that as soon as you begin to inquire into the nature of these actors – real players pretending to be spirits, pretending to be actors, pretending to be goddesses, as E. M. W. Tillyard once remarked – the overlay of illusions acquires a complexity like that of Pirandello. Essentially, however, there is an order. The trouble with it is that it is set up only to be destroyed. When Prospero points out at the end that there is no essential difference between this 'insubstantial pageant faded' (IV.1.155) and reality itself, he confounds entities normally thought of as distinct. He identifies the world with the stage, undercutting the sense of superiority usually felt by a theatre audience.

Up to this point in *The Tempest*, despite the bewildering superimposition of illusion upon illusion, the strangeness of the play as a whole, it has been possible to argue that the shifting nature of reality on the island is not a universal condition. It is a special state of affairs created by Prospero's art. In the maze of a formal garden, or an amusement park, one remains confident, despite checks and bewilderments, in the consciousness that this is only a game, that a logical world continues to exist outside it and will be reached at last. In much this manner, the audience is invited to cling to the details of past misgovernment at Milan, to the troubled relations of that dukedom with Naples, even to the marriage of Claribel at Tunis. Here sanity and certainty lie. What Prospero's fourth-Act speech does is to annihilate precisely this world outside the island which has hitherto encouraged trust: the world to which the characters of *The Tempest* plan to return at the end of the play, and which the theatre audience instinctively identifies with its own reality:

> *And, like the baseless fabric of this vision,*
> *The cloud-capped towers, the gorgeous palaces,*
> *The solemn temples, the great globe itself,*
> *Yea, all which it inherit, shall dissolve,*
> *And like this insubstantial pageant faded,*
> *Leave not a rack behind. We are such stuff*
> *As dreams are made on; and our little life*
> *Is rounded with a sleep.*   IV.1.151-8

The reality of life beyond the confines of the island, and also of life outside the doors of the theatre, is here equated with the transitory existence of the play-within-the-play. It is no more solid than, no different from, that tissue of illusion which has just vanished so completely, dissolved into nothingness at the bidding of Prospero.

At the very end, Prospero is given the task of dissolving another imaginative construct, one far larger and more complex than the masque of Iris and Ceres. As Epilogue, it is his duty to admit that the play world now lies in ruins, and to appeal for grace to the superior reality of that theatre audience which, for a little while, has submitted itself to the illusion of *The Tempest*. Elizabethan plays customarily humble themselves in some such manner at the end. They plead for applause, try to please with a dance, or, in tragedy, admit their artificiality by the mechanical necessity of bearing off their dead. An epilogue like the one which concludes *All's Well that Ends Well* is fairly typical.

> *The King's a beggar, now the play is done.*
> *All is well ended if this suit be won,*
> *That you express content ; which we will pay*
> *With strife to please you, day exceeding day.*
> *Ours be your patience then, and yours our parts ;*
> *Your gentle hands lend us, and take our hearts.*

Here, Shakespeare had played quite straightforwardly with the duality of actor and part, the King of France in his majesty reduced to a poor player, begging for favour and applause. In the speech, two worlds were juxtaposed sharply: active and passive, fictional and real. The end of the play, the shattering of illusion, were emphasized.

This is not, however, what happens in the epilogue to *The Tempest*. Prospero does not cease to be Prospero in the moment that he turns to address the theatre audience, does not step out of the illusion of the play. Instead, he does something far more in keeping with that identification of stage world with real world which he had made at the end of the masque in Act IV: he blurs planes of reality which are ordinarily distinct. Like most Epilogues, Prospero asks for applause. He asks for it, however, not with the voice of an actor merely but as Prospero himself, still in character, but suddenly and mysteriously aware of the theatre audience and of the conditions of performance.

> *Now 'tis true*
> *I must be here confined by you,*
> *Or sent to Naples. Let me not,*
> *Since I have my dukedom got*

And pardoned the deceiver, dwell
In this bare island by your spell;
But release me from my bands
With the help of your good hands.

This is not the simple utterance of a player constructing
a parallel between his *persona* in the play and his real self.
Rather, it is a deliberate drawing together of audience and
actor. Prospero begs release not from a stage, but from the
island. He wishes to return to his dukedom, not simply to
the tiring-house. The play may be done, but he is no
ordinary beggar for applause, admitting the ruin of illusion.
The epilogue actually perpetuates this illusion and firmly,
if with great deference and courtesy, involves the audience
with it. The effect is to suggest that the play goes on
beyond the formal limits of its fifth Act, that it runs into
and shares the reality of its audience. This is the last of the
surprises which *The Tempest* has to offer, the last of its
reminders that it stands on a frontier of what is possible
in the theatre. Speculation about Shakespeare's silence in
his final years is always unsatisfactory. It may be, however, that *The Tempest* was his last play because in it even
he had reached the point beyond which there could be no
further dramatic development.

FURTHER READING

The most comprehensively edited texts of the play are Frank Kermode's Arden (1954) and Stephen Orgel's Oxford (1987). Although Kermode's Introduction has rightly been widely admired for its formidable intelligence and breadth of reading, it suffers somewhat from his reluctance to consider the play in the theatre. His *Shakespeare: The Final Plays* (1963) offers a partial explanation for this omission in its discussion of Shakespeare's interest in romance at the end of his career: 'the most profitable explanation is that which postulates a revival of theatrical interest in romance, and seeks the reason for it not so much in the older drama as in the great heroic romances of the period, Sidney's *Arcadia* and Spenser's *Faerie Queene*.' Notable book-length treatments of Shakespeare's re-aroused interest in romance include Howard Felperin's indispensable *Shakespearean Romance* (1972), which sees Shakespeare's reworkings of classical and chivalric romance as imbued with the spirit of a besieged Protestantism, and Northrop Frye's *A Natural Perspective: The Development of Shakespearean Comedy and Romance* (1955).

Unlike Kermode's, Stephen Orgel's Oxford edition is intensely interested in the play as a theatrical experience, and is particularly helpful in showing the relationship between *The Tempest* and the 'civilising vision' of the court masque. It also explores the importance of the *Aenid* to an understanding of the play and its connection with epic. Orgel is also very astute, as some other recent critics have been, in assessing the play's political significance. Among other insights, he notes that Miranda's acceptance of Ferdinand's cheating makes it clear that 'Italian *Realpolitik* is already established in the next generation'. Her marriage to Ferdinand is not just a love-match but a political act. It excludes Antonio from any future claim on the ducal throne, but it also disposes of the realm as a political entity - Milan will become part of Naples. Prospero hasn't so much regained his kingdom, Orgel believes, as usurped his brother's.

As Orgel also points out, recent criticism has emphasized, and by and large been delighted by, the play's quirkiness. The paradigm for this response is Harry Berger's 'Miraculous Harp: A Reading of Shakespeare's *Tempest*' in *Shakespeare Studies* 5 (1969). In this quite masterly exercise of imaginative integration, Berger reveals the sometimes startling resemblances between Prospero, Ariel, Sycorax, Caliban and Gonzalo. His comment on Claribel's forced marriage to the Prince of Tunis is a good example of his eloquent awareness of the larger cultural significance of the play's events; in this marriage, as in the play as a whole, we see 'the civilized European soul compromising with darkness, surrendering its clear-beautiful ideals for the sake of expediency, and thereby reversing the forward direction of western man's ardous Virgilian journey'. These Virgilian echoes, so teasing for Orgel and Berger, are exhaustively explored in Donna B. Hamilton's *Virgil and 'The Tempest': the Politics of Imitation* (1990), in which she claims that there are two authorities for the play: Virgil and James I. The book pursues the Virgilian authority, exploring the Bloomian notion that in *The Tempest* Shakespeare is 'asserting himself over the poet whom he had confronted and rewritten almost obsessively throughout his career'.

For many critics the quirkiness of *The Tempest* is a mixed blessing. D. G. James's essay 'The Failure of the Ballad-Makers', for instance, in his book *Scepticism and Poetry: An Essay on the Poetic Imagination* (1937), is a meditation on the meditativeness of the Last Plays, in which *The Tempest* is a dramatic failure in its attempt to convey 'the myth of lost and recovered royalty'. In his more detailed excursion into what he calls *The Dream of Prospero* (1967), James argues that in the play 'we behold . . . the mind of Europe saying farewell to magic as part of its imagination of the world'. In a desperate interpretative move, James himself bids farewell to the play's

53

reality by claiming its events to be figments of Prospero's imagination: what we witness is Prospero's dream. Tougher-minded critics, perhaps, are more accepting of the troubling reality of the play. In some cases, as in Jan Kott's essay 'Prospero's Staff' in *Shakespeare Our Contemporary* (1964), there seems to be an exclusive and hence misleading pandering to the play's brutal and nihilistic elements. A more balanced view can be found in A. D. Nuttall's 'Two Unassimilable Men' in *Shakespearian Comedy* (1972), in which he argues that 'Prospero belongs not in the ethically warm universe of Christianity but in the hard, bright, far-off world of Greek legend with its demons, sun, sea and mortality.' The play's ending, he argues, is 'sick with ambiguity'. David L. Hirst, in a superior example of the Text and Performance Series (1984), echoes this judgement and has an excellent discussion of what exactly Prospero's project is. *The Tempest* itself 'is a play about power'.

For some of these unsentimental critics the ethically warm universe of Christianity has been replaced in the play by a world of colonial exploitation. Paul Brown's essay ' "This thing of darkness I acknowledge mine": *The Tempest* and the Discourse of Colonialism' in *Political Shakespeare* (1985) talks of Shakespeare's 'patronal' relationships with prominent members of the Virginia Company and sees Prospero's treatment of the indigenous inhabitants of the island as analogous to, not to say allegorical of, the savage paternalism of the British in Ireland. Stephen Greenblatt's essay 'Learning to Curse: Aspects of Linguistic Colonialism in the Sixteenth Century' in *First Images of America* (1976) takes the same line and also argues that '*The Tempest* utterly rejects the uniformitarian view of the human race, the view that would later triumph in the Enlightenment and prevail in the West to this day.' Essays of this stripe should be read in the stimulating company of Stephen Orgel's other work on *The Tempest*: 'Prospero's Wife' in *Rewriting the Renaissance: The Discourses of Sexual Difference in Early Modern Europe* (1986), 'Shakespeare and the Cannibals' in *Cannibals, Witches and Divorce* (1987), and 'New Uses of Adversity: Tragic

Experience in *The Tempest*' in *In Defence of Reading* (1963). 'Prospero's Wife' is a particularly powerful essay, in which Orgel argues that the absence of Prospero's wife is symptomatic of the 'absent, the unspoken ... the most powerful and problematic presence in *The Tempest*'. Despite the fact that, like any other Shakespeare comedy, the play moves towards an inevitable marriage, 'the relations it postulates between men and women are ignorant at best, characteristically tense, and potentially tragic'.

Whither has fled criticism's traditional visionary gleam about *The Tempest*? Utopian (mis)understandings of the play (once so popular) are now – no doubt rightly – out of favour. Not entirely so, however, as Gary Schmidgall's *Shakespeare and the Courtly Aesthetic* (1981) testifies. Despite his assertion of the profoundly ambiguous nature of the play – for example, does Prospero intend all along to forgive his enemies? – Schmidgall insists that *The Tempest* and the other Last Plays celebrate an 'astonishing recovery of political optimism'. Unlike Marston at the end of *his* working life, Schmidgall contends, Shakespeare refused to 'sequester himself in misanthropy', and *The Tempest* amounts to a political *summum bonum*' in which there is a 'yearning for peace, dynastic continuity, union, social concord, and "use of service"'. *The Tempest* should be compared with Book 6 of the *Faerie Queene*: in both there is the 'conquest of civic monsters by idealized courtiers'; Calidore and Ferdinand are 'idealized courtly neophytes'. He concludes: '*Hamlet* and *King Lear* are Shakespeare's most Montaignesque dramas, *The Tempest* is his most Baconian.' David Daniell in The Critics Debate Series (1989) has interesting things to say about the internationalism of this courtly context, and asks the provocatively unanswerable question, 'Does it stand first [in the 1623 Folio] because it points the way to read all Shakespeare?' And in a fascinating essay, 'Shakespeare's Final View of Women' in the *Times Literary Supplement* of 30 November 1979, D. W. Harding considers the mutually beneficent relationship between daughters and fathers in the Last Plays, climaxing in *The Tempest*: 'In this mature relation between father and daughter the fourth play thus ends with the greatest possible contrast to the incestuous relation at Antioch with which the first [*Pericles*] began.'

The variety – and vagaries – of these responses to *The Tempest* can be sampled in a number of essay collections: D. J. Palmer's Casebook (1968), for example, and Hallett Smith's Twentieth Century Interpretations (1969). John Russell Brown has a useful introduction in the Studies in English Literature Series (1969), and Harold Bloom has edited a book of essays devoted to Caliban (1992), that magnetic conundrum for critics. Despite his mere 177 lines (as opposed to Prospero's 653), Alden T. Vaughan and Virginia Mason, a historian and a Shakespearean, devote a book to him, *Shakespeare's Caliban: A Cultural History* (1991).

Michael Taylor, 1996

THE TEMPEST

THE CHARACTERS IN THE PLAY

ALONSO, King of Naples
SEBASTIAN, his brother
PROSPERO, the right Duke of Milan
ANTONIO, his brother, the usurping Duke of Milan
FERDINAND, son of the King of Naples
GONZALO, an honest old councillor
ADRIAN
FRANCISCO } lords
CALIBAN, a savage and deformed slave
TRINCULO, a jester
STEPHANO, a drunken butler
Master of a ship
Boatswain
Mariners
MIRANDA, daughter of Prospero
ARIEL, an airy spirit
IRIS
CERES
JUNO } characters in the masque, played by Ariel and
Nymphs } other Spirits
Reapers

Additional Spirits in the service of Prospero

A tempestuous noise of thunder and lightning heard
Enter a Shipmaster and a Boatswain

MASTER Boatswain!

BOATSWAIN Here, Master. What cheer?

MASTER Good. Speak to th'mariners. Fall to't, yarely, or we run ourselves aground. Bestir, bestir! *Exit*
Enter Mariners

BOATSWAIN Heigh, my hearts! Cheerly, cheerly, my hearts! Yare, yare! Take in the topsail! Tend to th'Master's whistle! – Blow till thou burst thy wind, if room enough.
Enter Alonso, Sebastian, Antonio, Ferdinand, Gonzalo, and others

ALONSO Good Boatswain, have care. Where's the Master? Play the men.   10

BOATSWAIN I pray now, keep below.

ANTONIO Where is the Master, Boatswain?

BOATSWAIN Do you not hear him? You mar our labour. Keep your cabins! You do assist the storm.

GONZALO Nay, good, be patient.

BOATSWAIN When the sea is. Hence! What cares these roarers for the name of king? To cabin! Silence! Trouble us not.

GONZALO Good, yet remember whom thou hast aboard.

BOATSWAIN None that I more love than myself. You are 20 a councillor. If you can command these elements to silence, and work the peace of the present, we will not hand a rope more. Use your authority. If you cannot,

give thanks you have lived so long, and make yourself
ready in your cabin for the mischance of the hour, if it
so hap. – Cheerly, good hearts! – Out of our way, I
say!   *Exit*

GONZALO I have great comfort from this fellow. Methinks he hath no drowning-mark upon him: his com-
30   plexion is perfect gallows. Stand fast, good Fate, to his
hanging. Make the rope of his destiny our cable, for
our own doth little advantage. If he be not born to be
hanged, our case is miserable.

                           Exeunt Gonzalo and the other nobles
                  Enter Boatswain

BOATSWAIN Down with the topmast! Yare! Lower,
lower! Bring her to try with main-course.

                  A cry within

A plague upon this howling! They are louder than the
weather, or our office.

                  Enter Sebastian, Antonio, and Gonzalo

Yet again? What do you here? Shall we give o'er and
drown? Have you a mind to sink?

40 SEBASTIAN A pox o'your throat, you bawling, blasphemous, incharitable dog!

BOATSWAIN Work you, then.

ANTONIO Hang, cur, hang, you whoreson, insolent noise-
maker! We are less afraid to be drowned than thou art.

GONZALO I'll warrant him for drowning, though the ship
were no stronger than a nutshell and as leaky as an
unstanched wench.

BOATSWAIN Lay her a-hold, a-hold! Set her two courses!
Off to sea again! Lay her off!

                  Enter Mariners wet

50 MARINERS All lost! To prayers, to prayers! All lost!

                                                                      Exeunt

BOATSWAIN What, must our mouths be cold?

GONZALO

    The King and Prince at prayers, let's assist them,
For our case is as theirs.

SEBASTIAN   I'm out of patience.

ANTONIO

    We are merely cheated of our lives by drunkards.
This wide-chopped rascal – would thou mightst lie
        drowning
The washing of ten tides!

GONZALO   He'll be hanged yet,
Though every drop of water swear against it,
And gape at wid'st to glut him.

        A confused noise within: 'Mercy on us!' – 'We
        split, we split!' – 'Farewell, my wife and children!'
        – 'Farewell, brother!' – 'We split, we split, we
        split!'   *Exit Boatswain*

ANTONIO Let's all sink wi'th'King.

SEBASTIAN Let's take leave of him.   *Exit, with Antonio* 60

GONZALO Now would I give a thousand furlongs of sea
    for an acre of barren ground. Long heath, brown furze,
    anything. The wills above be done, but I would fain die
    a dry death.   *Exit*

       Enter Prospero and Miranda   I.2

MIRANDA

    If by your art, my dearest father, you have
Put the wild waters in this roar, allay them.
The sky it seems would pour down stinking pitch,
But that the sea, mounting to th'welkin's cheek,
Dashes the fire out. O, I have suffered
With those that I saw suffer! A brave vessel,
Who had, no doubt, some noble creature in her,
Dashed all to pieces. O, the cry did knock

Against my very heart! Poor souls, they perished.
Had I been any god of power, I would
Have sunk the sea within the earth, or ere
It should the good ship so have swallowed and
The fraughting souls within her.

PROSPERO   Be collected.
No more amazement. Tell your piteous heart
There's no harm done.

MIRANDA   O, woe the day!

PROSPERO   No harm.
I have done nothing but in care of thee,
Of thee, my dear one, thee my daughter, who
Art ignorant of what thou art, naught knowing
Of whence I am, nor that I am more better
Than Prospero, master of a full poor cell,
And thy no greater father.

MIRANDA   More to know
Did never meddle with my thoughts.

PROSPERO   'Tis time
I should inform thee farther. Lend thy hand,
And pluck my magic garment from me. – So,
Lie there, my art. – Wipe thou thine eyes. Have comfort.
The direful spectacle of the wrack, which touched
The very virtue of compassion in thee,
I have with such provision in mine art
So safely ordered, that there is no soul –
No, not so much perdition as an hair
Betid to any creature in the vessel
Which thou heard'st cry, which thou sawst sink. Sit
          down.
For thou must now know farther.

MIRANDA   You have often
Begun to tell me what I am, but stopped,
And left me to a bootless inquisition,

Concluding, 'Stay: not yet.'

PROSPERO   The hour's now come.

The very minute bids thee ope thine ear.

Obey, and be attentive. Canst thou remember

A time before we came unto this cell?

I do not think thou canst, for then thou wast not   40

Out three years old.

MIRANDA   Certainly, sir, I can.

PROSPERO

By what? By any other house or person?

Of any thing the image tell me, that

Hath kept with thy remembrance.

MIRANDA   'Tis far off,

And rather like a dream than an assurance

That my remembrance warrants. Had I not

Four or five women once that tended me?

PROSPERO

Thou hadst, and more, Miranda. But how is it

That this lives in thy mind? What seest thou else

In the dark backward and abysm of time?   50

If thou rememb'rest aught ere thou cam'st here,

How thou cam'st here thou mayst.

MIRANDA   But that I do not.

PROSPERO

Twelve year since, Miranda, twelve year since,

Thy father was the Duke of Milan and

A prince of power.

MIRANDA   Sir, are not you my father?

PROSPERO

Thy mother was a piece of virtue, and

She said thou wast my daughter; and thy father

Was Duke of Milan; and his only heir

And princess, no worse issued.

MIRANDA   O the heavens!

60   What foul play had we, that we came from thence?
Or blessèd was't we did?

PROSPERO   Both, both, my girl.
By foul play, as thou sayst, were we heaved thence,
But blessedly holp hither.

MIRANDA   O, my heart bleeds
To think o'th'teen that I have turned you to,
Which is from my remembrance! Please you, farther.

PROSPERO
My brother and thy uncle, called Antonio –
I pray thee mark me, that a brother should
Be so perfidious! – he, whom next thyself
Of all the world I loved, and to him put

70   The manage of my state, as at that time
Through all the signories it was the first,
And Prospero the prime duke, being so reputed
In dignity, and for the liberal arts
Without a parallel; those being all my study,
The government I cast upon my brother,
And to my state grew stranger, being transported
And rapt in secret studies. Thy false uncle –
Dost thou attend me?

MIRANDA   Sir, most heedfully.

PROSPERO
Being once perfected how to grant suits,

80   How to deny them, who t'advance, and who
To trash for over-topping, new created
The creatures that were mine, I say, or changed 'em,
Or else new formed 'em; having both the key
Of officer and office, set all hearts i'th'state
To what tune pleased his ear, that now he was
The ivy which had hid my princely trunk,
And sucked my verdure out on't. Thou attend'st not!

MIRANDA
O, good sir, I do.

PROSPERO   I pray thee, mark me.
I, thus neglecting worldly ends, all dedicated
To closeness and the bettering of my mind   90
With that which, but by being so retired,
O'er-prized all popular rate, in my false brother
Awaked an evil nature; and my trust,
Like a good parent, did beget of him
A falsehood in its contrary, as great
As my trust was, which had indeed no limit,
A confidence sans bound. He being thus lorded,
Not only with what my revenue yielded,
But what my power might else exact, like one
Who having into truth, by telling of it,   100
Made such a sinner of his memory
To credit his own lie, he did believe
He was indeed the Duke, out o'th'substitution
And executing th'outward face of royalty,
With all prerogative. Hence his ambition growing –
Dost thou hear?
MIRANDA   Your tale, sir, would cure deafness.
PROSPERO
To have no screen between this part he played
And him he played it for, he needs will be
Absolute Milan. Me, poor man, my library
Was dukedom large enough. Of temporal royalties   110
He thinks me now incapable, confederates –
So dry he was for sway – wi'th'King of Naples
To give him annual tribute, do him homage,
Subject his coronet to his crown, and bend
The dukedom yet unbowed – alas, poor Milan –
To most ignoble stooping.
MIRANDA   O the heavens!
PROSPERO
Mark his condition and th'event; then tell me
If this might be a brother.

MIRANDA   I should sin
To think but nobly of my grandmother.
120 Good wombs have borne bad sons.
PROSPERO   Now the condition.
This King of Naples, being an enemy
To me inveterate, hearkens my brother's suit,
Which was, that he, in lieu o'th'premises
Of homage and I know not how much tribute,
Should presently extirpate me and mine
Out of the dukedom, and confer fair Milan,
With all the honours, on my brother. Whereon,
A treacherous army levied, one midnight
Fated to th'purpose, did Antonio open
130 The gates of Milan; and, i'th'dead of darkness,
The ministers for th'purpose hurried thence
Me and thy crying self.
MIRANDA   Alack, for pity.
I, not remembering how I cried out then,
Will cry it o'er again. It is a hint
That wrings mine eyes to't.
PROSPERO   Hear a little further,
And then I'll bring thee to the present business
Which now's upon's; without the which, this story
Were most impertinent.
MIRANDA   Wherefore did they not
That hour destroy us?
PROSPERO   Well demanded, wench.
140 My tale provokes that question. Dear, they durst not,
So dear the love my people bore me; nor set
A mark so bloody on the business, but
With colours fairer painted their foul ends.
In few, they hurried us aboard a bark,
Bore us some leagues to sea, where they prepared
A rotten carcass of a butt, not rigged,

Nor tackle, sail, nor mast. The very rats
Instinctively have quit it. There they hoist us,
To cry to th'sea that roared to us, to sigh
To th'winds, whose pity sighing back again   150
Did us but loving wrong.

MIRANDA   Alack, what trouble
Was I then to you!

PROSPERO   O, a cherubin
Thou wast that did preserve me. Thou didst smile,
Infusèd with a fortitude from heaven,
When I have decked the sea with drops full salt,
Under my burden groaned, which raised in me
An undergoing stomach, to bear up
Against what should ensue.

MIRANDA   How came we ashore?

PROSPERO
By Providence divine.
Some food we had, and some fresh water, that   160
A noble Neapolitan, Gonzalo,
Out of his charity, who being then appointed
Master of this design, did give us, with
Rich garments, linens, stuffs, and necessaries
Which since have steaded much. So, of his gentleness,
Knowing I loved my books, he furnished me
From mine own library with volumes that
I prize above my dukedom.

MIRANDA   Would I might
But ever see that man!

PROSPERO   Now I arise.
Sit still, and hear the last of our sea-sorrow.   170
Here in this island we arrived, and here
Have I, thy schoolmaster, made thee more profit
Than other princess can, that have more time
For vainer hours, and tutors not so careful.

MIRANDA

Heavens thank you for't! And now, I pray you, sir,
For still 'tis beating in my mind, your reason
For raising this sea-storm?

PROSPERO   Know thus far forth.
By accident most strange, bountiful Fortune,
Now my dear lady, hath mine enemies
180   Brought to this shore; and by my prescience
I find my zenith doth depend upon
A most auspicious star, whose influence
If now I court not, but omit, my fortunes
Will ever after droop. Here cease more questions.
Thou art inclined to sleep. 'Tis a good dullness,
And give it way. I know thou canst not choose.
     Miranda sleeps
Come away, servant, come! I am ready now.
Approach, my Ariel! Come!
     Enter Ariel

ARIEL

All hail, great master! Grave sir, hail! I come
190   To answer thy best pleasure, be't to fly,
To swim, to dive into the fire, to ride
On the curled clouds. To thy strong bidding task
Ariel and all his quality.

PROSPERO   Hast thou, spirit,
Performed to point the tempest that I bade thee?

ARIEL

To every article.
I boarded the King's ship. Now on the beak,
Now in the waist, the deck, in every cabin
I flamed amazement. Sometime I'd divide,
And burn in many places. On the topmast,
200   The yards, and boresprit would I flame distinctly,
Then meet and ioin. Jove's lightnings, the precursors

O'th'dreadful thunderclaps, more momentary
And sight-outrunning were not. The fire and cracks
Of sulphurous roaring the most mighty Neptune
Seem to besiege, and make his bold waves tremble,
Yea, his dread trident shake.

PROSPERO   My brave spirit!
Who was so firm, so constant, that this coil
Would not infect his reason?

ARIEL   Not a soul
But felt a fever of the mad, and played
Some tricks of desperation. All but mariners   210
Plunged in the foaming brine, and quit the vessel,
Then all afire with me. The King's son Ferdinand,
With hair up-staring — then like reeds, not hair —
Was the first man that leaped; cried, 'Hell is empty,
And all the devils are here!'

PROSPERO   Why, that's my spirit!
But was not this nigh shore?

ARIEL   Close by, my master.

PROSPERO
But are they, Ariel, safe?

ARIEL   Not a hair perished.
On their sustaining garments not a blemish,
But fresher than before; and as thou bad'st me,
In troops I have dispersed them 'bout the isle.   220
The King's son have I landed by himself,
Whom I left cooling of the air with sighs
In an odd angle of the isle, and sitting,
His arms in this sad knot.

PROSPERO   Of the King's ship,
The mariners, say how thou hast disposed,
And all the rest o'th'fleet?

ARIEL   Safely in harbour
Is the King's ship, in the deep nook where once

Thou called'st me up at midnight to fetch dew
From the still-vexed Bermoothes, there she's hid;
230   The mariners all under hatches stowed,
Who, with a charm joined to their suffered labour,
I have left asleep. And for the rest o'th'fleet,
Which I dispersed, they all have met again,
And are upon the Mediterranean flote
Bound sadly home for Naples,
Supposing that they saw the King's ship wracked,
And his great person perish.

PROSPERO   Ariel, thy charge
Exactly is performed, but there's more work.
What is the time o'th'day?

ARIEL   Past the mid-season.

PROSPERO
240   At least two glasses. The time 'twixt six and now
Must by us both be spent most preciously.

ARIEL
Is there more toil? Since thou dost give me pains,
Let me remember thee what thou hast promised,
Which is not yet performed me.

PROSPERO   How now? Moody?
What is't thou canst demand?

ARIEL   My liberty.

PROSPERO
Before the time be out? No more.

ARIEL   I prithee,
Remember I have done thee worthy service,
Told thee no lies, made thee no mistakings, served
Without or grudge or grumblings. Thou did promise
250   To bate me a full year.

PROSPERO   Dost thou forget
From what a torment I did free thee?

ARIEL   No.

PROSPERO

    Thou dost; and think'st it much to tread the ooze
    Of the salt deep,
    To run upon the sharp wind of the north,
    To do me business in the veins o'th'earth
    When it is baked with frost.

ARIEL   I do not, sir.

PROSPERO

    Thou liest, malignant thing! Hast thou forgot
    The foul witch Sycorax, who with age and envy
    Was grown into a hoop? Hast thou forgot her?

ARIEL

    No, sir.

PROSPERO

            Thou hast. Where was she born? Speak! Tell me! 260

ARIEL

    Sir, in Argier.

PROSPERO   O, was she so! I must
    Once in a month recount what thou hast been,
    Which thou forget'st. This damned witch Sycorax,
    For mischiefs manifold, and sorceries terrible
    To enter human hearing, from Argier,
    Thou know'st, was banished. For one thing she did
    They would not take her life. Is not this true?

ARIEL

    Ay, sir.

PROSPERO

    This blue-eyed hag was hither brought with child,
    And here was left by th'sailors. Thou, my slave,   270
    As thou report'st thyself, was then her servant.
    And for thou wast a spirit too delicate
    To act her earthy and abhorred commands,
    Refusing her grand hests, she did confine thee,
    By help of her more potent ministers,

And in her most unmitigable rage,
Into a cloven pine; within which rift
Imprisoned, thou didst painfully remain
A dozen years, within which space she died,
And left thee there, where thou didst vent thy groans
As fast as millwheels strike. Then was this island –
Save for the son that she did litter here,
A freckled whelp, hag-born – not honoured with
A human shape.

ARIEL   Yes, Caliban her son.

PROSPERO
Dull thing, I say so! He, that Caliban
Whom now I keep in service. Thou best know'st
What torment I did find thee in. Thy groans
Did make wolves howl, and penetrate the breasts
Of ever-angry bears. It was a torment
To lay upon the damned, which Sycorax
Could not again undo. It was mine art,
When I arrived and heard thee, that made gape
The pine, and let thee out.

ARIEL   I thank thee, master.

PROSPERO
If thou more murmur'st, I will rend an oak,
And peg thee in his knotty entrails, till
Thou hast howled away twelve winters.

ARIEL   Pardon, master.
I will be correspondent to command,
And do my spriting gently.

PROSPERO   Do so, and after two days
I will discharge thee.

ARIEL   That's my noble master!
What shall I do? Say what! What shall I do?

PROSPERO
Go make thyself like a nymph o'th'sea.

74

Be subject to no sight but thine and mine, invisible
To every eyeball else. Go take this shape,
And hither come in't. Go! Hence with diligence!

                                        Exit Ariel

Awake, dear heart, awake! Thou hast slept well.
Awake!

MIRANDA The strangeness of your story put
Heaviness in me.

PROSPERO   Shake it off. Come on;
We'll visit Caliban, my slave, who never
Yields us kind answer.

MIRANDA   'Tis a villain, sir,
I do not love to look on.

PROSPERO   But, as 'tis,   310
We cannot miss him. He does make our fire,
Fetch in our wood, and serves in offices
That profit us. What, ho! Slave! Caliban!
Thou earth, thou, speak!

CALIBAN (*within*)   There's wood enough within.

PROSPERO

Come forth, I say! There's other business for thee.
Come, thou tortoise! When?
        Enter Ariel like a water-nymph
Fine apparition! My quaint Ariel,
Hark in thine ear.

ARIEL   My lord, it shall be done.   *Exit*

PROSPERO

Thou poisonous slave, got by the devil himself
Upon thy wicked dam, come forth!   320
        Enter Caliban

CALIBAN

As wicked dew as e'er my mother brushed
With raven's feather from unwholesome fen
Drop on you both. A south-west blow on ye

75

And blister you all o'er.

PROSPERO

For this, be sure, tonight thou shalt have cramps,
Side-stitches that shall pen thy breath up. Urchins
Shall for that vast of night that they may work
All exercise on thee. Thou shalt be pinched
As thick as honey-comb, each pinch more stinging
330   Than bees that made 'em.

CALIBAN   I must eat my dinner.
This island's mine, by Sycorax my mother,
Which thou tak'st from me. When thou cam'st first,
Thou strok'st me, and made much of me, wouldst give
    me
Water with berries in't, and teach me how
To name the bigger light, and how the less,
That burn by day and night. And then I loved thee,
And showed thee all the qualities o'th'isle,
The fresh springs, brine-pits, barren place and fertile.
Cursed be I that did so! All the charms
340   Of Sycorax – toads, beetles, bats light on you!
For I am all the subjects that you have,
Which first was mine own king; and here you sty me
In this hard rock, whiles you do keep from me
The rest o'th'island.

PROSPERO   Thou most lying slave,
Whom stripes may move, not kindness! I have used
    thee,
Filth as thou art, with human care, and lodged thee
In mine own cell, till thou didst seek to violate
The honour of my child.

CALIBAN

O ho, O ho! Would't had been done!
350   Thou didst prevent me. I had peopled else
This isle with Calibans.

MIRANDA   Abhorrèd slave,
  Which any print of goodness wilt not take,
  Being capable of all ill! I pitied thee,
  Took pains to make thee speak, taught thee each hour
  One thing or other. When thou didst not, savage,
  Know thine own meaning, but wouldst gabble like
  A thing most brutish, I endowed thy purposes
  With words that made them known. But thy vile race,
  Though thou didst learn, had that in't which good
            natures
  Could not abide to be with. Therefore wast thou   360
  Deservedly confined into this rock, who hadst
  Deserved more than a prison.

CALIBAN
  You taught me language, and my profit on't
  Is, I know how to curse. The red plague rid you
  For learning me your language!

PROSPERO   Hag-seed, hence!
  Fetch us in fuel – and be quick, thou'rt best,
  To answer other business. Shrug'st thou, malice?
  If thou neglect'st, or dost unwillingly
  What I command, I'll rack thee with old cramps,
  Fill all thy bones with aches, make thee roar,   370
  That beasts shall tremble at thy din.

CALIBAN   No, pray thee!
  (aside) I must obey. His art is of such power,
  It would control my dam's god Setebos,
  And make a vassal of him.

PROSPERO   So, slave. Hence! Exit Caliban
        Enter Ferdinand; and Ariel, invisible, playing and
        singing

ARIEL   Song
                Come unto these yellow sands,
                    And then take hands.

> Curtsied when you have and kissed
>   The wild waves whist,
> Foot it featly here and there;
> And, sweet sprites, the burden bear.
>   Hark, hark!
> (*Burden, dispersedly*) Bow-wow!
>   The watch-dogs bark.
> (*Burden, dispersedly*) Bow-wow!
>   Hark, hark! I hear
> The strain of strutting chanticleer
> Cry cock-a-diddle-dow!

FERDINAND

Where should this music be? I'th'air or th'earth?
It sounds no more; and sure it waits upon
Some god o'th'island. Sitting on a bank,
Weeping again the King my father's wrack,
This music crept by me upon the waters,
Allaying both their fury and my passion
With its sweet air. Thence I have followed it,
Or it hath drawn me, rather. But 'tis gone.
No, it begins again.

ARIEL   *Song*

> Full fathom five thy father lies,
>   Of his bones are coral made;
> Those are pearls that were his eyes;
>   Nothing of him that doth fade,
> But doth suffer a sea-change
> Into something rich and strange.
> Sea-nymphs hourly ring his knell:
> (*Burden*) Ding-dong.
>   Hark! Now I hear them – Ding-dong bell.

FERDINAND

The ditty does remember my drowned father.
This is no mortal business, nor no sound

78

That the earth owes. I hear it now above me.

PROSPERO

The fringèd curtains of thine eye advance,
And say what thou seest yond.

MIRANDA   What is't? A spirit?   410
Lord, how it looks about! Believe me, sir,
It carries a brave form. But 'tis a spirit.

PROSPERO

No, wench. It eats and sleeps and hath such senses
As we have, such. This gallant which thou seest
Was in the wrack; and, but he's something stained
With grief, that's beauty's canker, thou mightst call him
A goodly person. He hath lost his fellows,
And strays about to find 'em.

MIRANDA   I might call him
A thing divine, for nothing natural
I ever saw so noble.

PROSPERO (aside)   It goes on, I see,   420
As my soul prompts it. – Spirit, fine spirit, I'll free thee
Within two days for this!

FERDINAND   Most sure, the goddess
On whom these airs attend! Vouchsafe my prayer
May know if you remain upon this island,
And that you will some good instruction give
How I may bear me here. My prime request,
Which I do last pronounce, is – O you wonder! –
If you be maid or no?

MIRANDA   No wonder, sir,
But certainly a maid.

FERDINAND   My language? Heavens!
I am the best of them that speak this speech,   430
Were I but where 'tis spoken.

PROSPERO   How? The best?
What wert thou if the King of Naples heard thee?

FERDINAND

    A single thing, as I am now, that wonders
    To hear thee speak of Naples. He does hear me,
    And that he does, I weep. Myself am Naples,
    Who with mine eyes, never since at ebb, beheld
    The King my father wracked.

MIRANDA   Alack, for mercy!

FERDINAND

    Yes, faith, and all his lords, the Duke of Milan
    And his brave son being twain.

PROSPERO (*aside*)   The Duke of Milan

440   And his more braver daughter could control thee,
    If now 'twere fit to do't. At the first sight
    They have changed eyes. Delicate Ariel,
    I'll set thee free for this. – A word, good sir.
    I fear you have done yourself some wrong. A word!

MIRANDA

    Why speaks my father so ungently? This
    Is the third man that e'er I saw; the first
    That e'er I sighed for. Pity move my father
    To be inclined my way.

FERDINAND   O, if a virgin,
    And your affection not gone forth, I'll make you

450   The Queen of Naples.

PROSPERO   Soft, sir! One word more.
    (*aside*) They are both in either's powers. But this swift
           business
    I must uneasy make, lest too light winning
    Make the prize light. – One word more! I charge thee
    That thou attend me. Thou dost here usurp
    The name thou ow'st not, and hast put thyself
    Upon this island as a spy, to win it
    From me, the lord on't.

FERDINAND   No, as I am a man!

MIRANDA

There's nothing ill can dwell in such a temple.
If the ill spirit have so fair a house,
Good things will strive to dwell with't.

PROSPERO   Follow me.   460

(*to Miranda*) Speak not you for him. He's a traitor. –
   Come!
I'll manacle thy neck and feet together.
Sea-water shalt thou drink; thy food shall be
The fresh-brook mussels, withered roots, and husks
Wherein the acorn cradled. Follow!

FERDINAND   No!

I will resist such entertainment till
Mine enemy has more power.

He draws, and is charmed from moving

MIRANDA   O dear father,

Make not too rash a trial of him, for
He's gentle, and not fearful.

PROSPERO   What, I say,

My foot my tutor? – Put thy sword up, traitor,   470
Who mak'st a show, but dar'st not strike, thy conscience
Is so possessed with guilt. Come from thy ward!
For I can here disarm thee with this stick,
And make thy weapon drop.

MIRANDA   Beseech you, father!

PROSPERO

Hence! Hang not on my garments.

MIRANDA   Sir, have pity.

I'll be his surety.

PROSPERO   Silence! One word more

Shall make me chide thee, if not hate thee. What,
An advocate for an impostor? Hush!
Thou think'st there is no more such shapes as he,
Having seen but him and Caliban. Foolish wench!   480

To th'most of men this is a Caliban,
And they to him are angels.

MIRANDA   My affections
Are then most humble. I have no ambition
To see a goodlier man.

PROSPERO   Come on, obey!
Thy nerves are in their infancy again,
And have no vigour in them.

FERDINAND   So they are.
My spirits, as in a dream, are all bound up.
My father's loss, the weakness which I feel,
The wrack of all my friends, nor this man's threats
490 To whom I am subdued, are but light to me,
Might I but through my prison once a day
Behold this maid. All corners else o'th'earth
Let liberty make use of. Space enough
Have I in such a prison.

PROSPERO (aside)   It works. (to Ferdinand) Come on. –
Thou hast done well, fine Ariel! (to Ferdinand) Follow me.
(to Ariel)
Hark what thou else shalt do me.

MIRANDA   Be of comfort.
My father's of a better nature, sir,
Than he appears by speech. This is unwonted
Which now came from him.

PROSPERO (to Ariel)   Thou shalt be as free
500 As mountain winds; but then exactly do
All points of my command.

ARIEL   To th'syllable.

PROSPERO
Come, follow! (to Miranda) Speak not for him. Exeunt

*

Enter Alonso, Sebastian, Antonio, Gonzalo, Adrian,
Francisco, and others

GONZALO
Beseech you, sir, be merry. You have cause –
So have we all – of joy; for our escape
Is much beyond our loss. Our hint of woe
Is common. Every day, some sailor's wife,
The masters of some merchant, and the merchant,
Have just our theme of woe. But for the miracle,
I mean our preservation, few in millions
Can speak like us. Then wisely, good sir, weigh
Our sorrow with our comfort.

ALONSO   Prithee, peace.

SEBASTIAN (*aside to Antonio*) He receives comfort like 10
cold porridge.

ANTONIO (*aside to Sebastian*) The visitor will not give
him o'er so.

SEBASTIAN (*aside to Antonio*) Look, he's winding up the
watch of his wit. By and by it will strike.

GONZALO Sir –

SEBASTIAN One: tell.

GONZALO
When every grief is entertained that's offered,
Comes to th'entertainer –

SEBASTIAN A dollar.   20

GONZALO Dolour comes to him indeed. You have spoken
truer than you purposed.

SEBASTIAN You have taken it wiselier than I meant you
should.

GONZALO (*to Alonso*) Therefore, my lord –

ANTONIO Fie, what a spendthrift is he of his tongue!

ALONSO I prithee, spare.

GONZALO Well, I have done. But yet –

SEBASTIAN He will be talking.

30 ANTONIO Which, of he or Adrian, for a good wager, first begins to crow?

SEBASTIAN The old cock.

ANTONIO The cockerel.

SEBASTIAN Done. The wager?

ANTONIO A laughter.

SEBASTIAN A match.

ADRIAN Though this island seem to be desert –

ANTONIO Ha, ha, ha!

SEBASTIAN So, you're paid.

40 ADRIAN Uninhabitable, and almost inaccessible –

SEBASTIAN Yet –

ADRIAN Yet –

ANTONIO He could not miss't.

ADRIAN It must needs be of subtle, tender, and delicate temperance.

ANTONIO Temperance was a delicate wench.

SEBASTIAN Ay, and a subtle, as he most learnedly delivered.

ADRIAN The air breathes upon us here most sweetly.

50 SEBASTIAN As if it had lungs, and rotten ones.

ANTONIO Or, as 'twere perfumed by a fen.

GONZALO Here is everything advantageous to life.

ANTONIO True, save means to live.

SEBASTIAN Of that there's none, or little.

GONZALO How lush and lusty the grass looks! How green!

ANTONIO The ground, indeed, is tawny.

SEBASTIAN With an eye of green in't.

ANTONIO He misses not much.

60 SEBASTIAN No. He doth but mistake the truth totally.

GONZALO But the rarity of it is – which is indeed almost beyond credit –

SEBASTIAN As many vouched rarities are.

GONZALO That our garments, being, as they were, drenched in the sea, hold, notwithstanding, their freshness and glosses, being rather new-dyed than stained with salt water.

ANTONIO If but one of his pockets could speak, would it not say he lies?

SEBASTIAN Ay, or very falsely pocket up his report. 70

GONZALO Methinks our garments are now as fresh as when we put them on first in Afric, at the marriage of the King's fair daughter Claribel to the King of Tunis.

SEBASTIAN 'Twas a sweet marriage, and we prosper well in our return.

ADRIAN Tunis was never graced before with such a paragon to their queen.

GONZALO Not since widow Dido's time.

ANTONIO Widow? A pox o' that! How came that widow in? Widow Dido! 80

SEBASTIAN What if he had said 'widower Aeneas' too? Good Lord, how you take it!

ADRIAN 'Widow Dido', said you? You make me study of that. She was of Carthage, not of Tunis.

GONZALO This Tunis, sir, was Carthage.

ADRIAN Carthage?

GONZALO I assure you, Carthage.

ANTONIO His word is more than the miraculous harp.

SEBASTIAN He hath raised the wall, and houses too.

ANTONIO What impossible matter will he make easy 90 next?

SEBASTIAN I think he will carry this island home in his pocket and give it his son for an apple.

ANTONIO And sowing the kernels of it in the sea, bring forth more islands.

GONZALO Ay.

ANTONIO Why, in good time.

GONZALO (*to Alonso*) Sir, we were talking, that our garments seem now as fresh as when we were at Tunis at
100   the marriage of your daughter, who is now Queen.

ANTONIO And the rarest that e'er came there.

SEBASTIAN Bate, I beseech you, widow Dido.

ANTONIO O, widow Dido? Ay, widow Dido.

GONZALO Is not, sir, my doublet as fresh as the first day
I wore it? I mean, in a sort.

ANTONIO That 'sort' was well fished for.

GONZALO When I wore it at your daughter's marriage.

ALONSO
You cram these words into mine ears against
The stomach of my sense. Would I had never
110   Married my daughter there! For, coming thence,
My son is lost, and, in my rate, she too,
Who is so far from Italy removed
I ne'er again shall see her. O thou mine heir
Of Naples and of Milan, what strange fish
Hath made his meal on thee?

FRANCISCO   Sir, he may live.
I saw him beat the surges under him,
And ride upon their backs. He trod the water,
Whose enmity he flung aside, and breasted
The surge most swoll'n that met him. His bold head
120   'Bove the contentious waves he kept, and oared
Himself with his good arms in lusty stroke
To th'shore, that o'er his wave-worn basis bowed,
As stooping to relieve him. I not doubt
He came alive to land.

ALONSO   No, no, he's gone.

SEBASTIAN
Sir, you may thank yourself for this great loss,
That would not bless our Europe with your daughter,
But rather loose her to an African,

Where she, at least, is banished from your eye,
Who hath cause to wet the grief on't.

ALONSO   Prithee, peace.

SEBASTIAN

You were kneeled to and importuned otherwise   130
By all of us; and the fair soul herself
Weighed between loathness and obedience at
Which end o'th'beam should bow. We have lost your
    son,
I fear, for ever. Milan and Naples have
More widows in them of this business' making
Than we bring men to comfort them.
The fault's your own.

ALONSO   So is the dear'st o'th'loss.

GONZALO

My lord Sebastian,
The truth you speak doth lack some gentleness,
And time to speak it in. You rub the sore,   140
When you should bring the plaster.

SEBASTIAN   Very well.

ANTONIO And most chirugeonly.

GONZALO (to Alonso)
It is foul weather in us all, good sir,
When you are cloudy.

SEBASTIAN (aside to Antonio)
                    Foul weather?

ANTONIO (aside to Sebastian)   Very foul.

GONZALO
Had I plantation of this isle, my lord –

ANTONIO (aside to Sebastian)
He'd sow't with nettle-seed.

SEBASTIAN (aside to Antonio) Or docks, or mallows.

GONZALO
And were the king on't, what would I do?

II.1

SEBASTIAN (*aside to Antonio*) 'Scape being drunk, for want of wine.

GONZALO

150 I'th'commonwealth I would by contraries
Execute all things. For no kind of traffic
Would I admit, no name of magistrate.
Letters should not be known. Riches, poverty,
And use of service, none. Contract, succession,
Bourn, bound of land, tilth, vineyard, none.
No use of metal, corn, or wine, or oil.
No occupation: all men idle, all,
And women too, but innocent and pure.
No sovereignty –

SEBASTIAN (*aside to Antonio*) Yet he would be king on't.

160 ANTONIO (*aside to Sebastian*) The latter end of his commonwealth forgets the beginning.

GONZALO

All things in common nature should produce
Without sweat or endeavour. Treason, felony,
Sword, pike, knife, gun, or need of any engine
Would I not have; but nature should bring forth
Of it own kind all foison, all abundance,
To feed my innocent people.

SEBASTIAN (*aside to Antonio*) No marrying 'mong his subjects?

170 ANTONIO (*aside to Sebastian*) None, man, all idle – whores and knaves.

GONZALO

I would with such perfection govern, sir,
T'excel the Golden Age.

SEBASTIAN   'Save his majesty!

ANTONIO

Long live Gonzalo!

GONZALO   And – do you mark me, sir?

ALONSO

    Prithee, no more. Thou dost talk nothing to me.

GONZALO I do well believe your highness, and did it to
    minister occasion to these gentlemen, who are of such
    sensible and nimble lungs that they always use to laugh
    at nothing.

ANTONIO 'Twas you we laughed at. 180

GONZALO Who, in this kind of merry fooling, am nothing
    to you; so you may continue, and laugh at nothing still.

ANTONIO What a blow was there given!

SEBASTIAN An it had not fall'n flat-long.

GONZALO You are gentlemen of brave mettle. You would
    lift the moon out of her sphere, if she would continue in
    it five weeks without changing.

    Enter Ariel, playing solemn music

SEBASTIAN We would so, and then go a-bat-fowling.

ANTONIO Nay, good my lord, be not angry.

GONZALO No, I warrant you, I will not adventure my 190
    discretion so weakly. Will you laugh me asleep, for I
    am very heavy?

ANTONIO Go sleep, and hear us.

    All sleep except Alonso, Sebastian, and Antonio

ALONSO

    What, all so soon asleep? I wish mine eyes
    Would, with themselves, shut up my thoughts. I find
    They are inclined to do so.

SEBASTIAN   Please you, sir,

    Do not omit the heavy offer of it.
    It seldom visits sorrow; when it doth,
    It is a comforter.

ANTONIO   We two, my lord,

    Will guard your person while you take your rest, 200
    And watch your safety.

ALONSO   Thank you. Wondrous heavy.

Alonso sleeps. Exit Ariel

SEBASTIAN

What a strange drowsiness possesses them!

ANTONIO

It is the quality o'th'climate.

SEBASTIAN   Why
Doth it not then our eyelids sink? I find
Not myself disposed to sleep.

ANTONIO

Nor I. My spirits are nimble.
They fell together all, as by consent.
They dropped, as by a thunderstroke. What might,
Worthy Sebastian? – O, what might? – No more!
And yet methinks I see it in thy face,
What thou shouldst be. Th'occasion speaks thee, and
My strong imagination sees a crown
Dropping upon thy head.

SEBASTIAN   What, art thou waking?

ANTONIO

Do you not hear me speak?

SEBASTIAN   I do, and surely
It is a sleepy language, and thou speak'st
Out of thy sleep. What is it thou didst say?
This is a strange repose, to be asleep
With eyes wide open; standing, speaking, moving,
And yet so fast asleep.

ANTONIO   Noble Sebastian,
Thou let'st thy fortune sleep – die, rather; wink'st
Whiles thou art waking.

SEBASTIAN   Thou dost snore distinctly.
There's meaning in thy snores.

ANTONIO

I am more serious than my custom. You
Must be so too, if heed me; which to do

90

Trebles thee o'er.

SEBASTIAN   Well, I am standing water.

ANTONIO

I'll teach you how to flow.

SEBASTIAN   Do so. To ebb

Hereditary sloth instructs me.

ANTONIO   O,

If you but knew how you the purpose cherish

Whiles thus you mock it! How, in stripping it,

You more invest it! Ebbing men, indeed,   230

Most often do so near the bottom run

By their own fear, or sloth.

SEBASTIAN   Prithee, say on.

The setting of thine eye and cheek proclaim

A matter from thee; and a birth, indeed,

Which throes thee much to yield.

ANTONIO   Thus, sir:

Although this lord of weak remembrance, this,

Who shall be of as little memory

When he is earthed, hath here almost persuaded –

For he's a spirit of persuasion, only

Professes to persuade – the King his son's alive,   240

'Tis as impossible that he's undrowned

As he that sleeps here swims.

SEBASTIAN   I have no hope

That he's undrowned.

ANTONIO   O, out of that no hope

What great hope have you! No hope that way is

Another way so high a hope that even

Ambition cannot pierce a wink beyond,

But doubt discovery there. Will you grant with me

That Ferdinand is drowned?

SEBASTIAN   He's gone.

ANTONIO   Then, tell me,

Who's the next heir of Naples?

SEBASTIAN   Claribel.

ANTONIO

250   She that is Queen of Tunis; she that dwells
Ten leagues beyond man's life; she that from Naples
Can have no note, unless the sun were post –
The Man i'th'Moon's too slow – till newborn chins
Be rough and razorable; she that from whom
We all were sea-swallowed, though some cast again,
And, by that destiny, to perform an act
Whereof what's past is prologue, what to come,
In yours and my discharge.

SEBASTIAN   What stuff is this?
How say you?

260   'Tis true my brother's daughter's Queen of Tunis,
So is she heir of Naples, 'twixt which regions
There is some space.

ANTONIO   A space whose ev'ry cubit
Seems to cry out, 'How shall that Claribel
Measure us back to Naples? Keep in Tunis,
And let Sebastian wake.' Say this were death
That now hath seized them, why, they were no worse
Than now they are. There be that can rule Naples
As well as he that sleeps; lords that can prate
As amply and unnecessarily

270   As this Gonzalo. I myself could make
A chough of as deep chat. O, that you bore
The mind that I do! What a sleep were this
For your advancement! Do you understand me?

SEBASTIAN

Methinks I do.

ANTONIO   And how does your content
Tender your own good fortune?

SEBASTIAN   I remember
You did supplant your brother Prospero.

ANTONIO   True.

And look how well my garments sit upon me,
Much feater than before. My brother's servants
Were then my fellows. Now they are my men.

SEBASTIAN

But, for your conscience?   280

ANTONIO

Ay, sir, where lies that? If 'twere a kibe,
'Twould put me to my slipper; but I feel not
This deity in my bosom. Twenty consciences
That stand 'twixt me and Milan, candied be they,
And melt ere they molest. Here lies your brother,
No better than the earth he lies upon,
If he were that which now he's like – that's dead –
Whom I with this obedient steel, three inches of it,
Can lay to bed for ever; whiles you, doing thus,
To the perpetual wink for aye might put   290
This ancient morsel, this Sir Prudence, who
Should not upbraid our course. For all the rest,
They'll take suggestion as a cat laps milk.
They'll tell the clock to any business that
We say befits the hour.

SEBASTIAN   Thy case, dear friend,

Shall be my precedent. As thou got'st Milan,
I'll come by Naples. Draw thy sword. One stroke
Shall free thee from the tribute which thou payest,
And I the King shall love thee.

ANTONIO   Draw together.

And when I rear my hand, do you the like,   300
To fall it on Gonzalo.

SEBASTIAN   O, but one word.

Enter Ariel with music and song

ARIEL

My master through his art foresees the danger
That you, his friend, are in, and sends me forth –

93

For else his project dies – to keep them living.
Sings in Gonzalo's ear

> While you here do snoring lie,
> Open-eyed conspiracy
>   His time doth take.
> If of life you keep a care,
> Shake off slumber, and beware.
>   Awake, awake!

ANTONIO

Then let us both be sudden.

GONZALO (*awakes*)   Now, good angels
Preserve the King!
The others awake

ALONSO

Why, how now? – Ho, awake! – Why are you drawn?
Wherefore this ghastly looking?

GONZALO   What's the matter?

SEBASTIAN

Whiles we stood here securing your repose,
Even now, we heard a hollow burst of bellowing
Like bulls, or rather lions. Did't not wake you?
It struck mine ear most terribly.

ALONSO   I heard nothing.

ANTONIO

O, 'twas a din to fright a monster's ear,
To make an earthquake! Sure it was the roar
Of a whole herd of lions.

ALONSO   Heard you this, Gonzalo?

GONZALO

Upon mine honour, sir, I heard a humming,
And that a strange one too, which did awake me.
I shaked you, sir, and cried. As mine eyes opened,
I saw their weapons drawn. There was a noise,
That's verily. 'Tis best we stand upon our guard,

Or that we quit this place. Let's draw our weapons.

ALONSO

Lead off this ground and let's make further search
For my poor son.

GONZALO   Heavens keep him from these beasts!
For he is sure i'th'island.

ALONSO   Lead away.   330

ARIEL

Prospero my lord shall know what I have done.
So, King, go safely on to seek thy son.   *Exeunt*

     Enter Caliban with a burden of wood. A noise of II.2
     thunder heard

CALIBAN

All the infections that the sun sucks up
From bogs, fens, flats, on Prosper fall, and make him
By inch-meal a disease! His spirits hear me,
And yet I needs must curse. But they'll nor pinch,
Fright me with urchin-shows, pitch me i'th'mire,
Nor lead me, like a firebrand, in the dark
Out of my way, unless he bid 'em. But
For every trifle are they set upon me;
Sometime like apes, that mow and chatter at me,
And after bite me; then like hedgehogs, which   10
Lie tumbling in my barefoot way, and mount
Their pricks at my footfall. Sometime am I
All wound with adders, who with cloven tongues
Do hiss me into madness.

    Enter Trinculo

                 Lo, now, lo!
Here comes a spirit of his, and to torment me
For bringing wood in slowly. I'll fall flat.
Perchance he will not mind me.

TRINCULO Here's neither bush nor shrub, to bear off
any weather at all, and another storm brewing. I hear it
20 sing i'th'wind. Yond same black cloud, yond huge one,
looks like a foul bombard that would shed his liquor. If
it should thunder as it did before, I know not where to
hide my head. Yond same cloud cannot choose but fall
by pailfuls. What have we here? A man or a fish? Dead
or alive? A fish! He smells like a fish; a very ancient and
fishlike smell; a kind of not-of-the-newest poor-John.
A strange fish! Were I in England now, as once I was,
and had but this fish painted, not a holiday fool there but
would give a piece of silver. There would this monster
30 make a man. Any strange beast there makes a man.
When they will not give a doit to relieve a lame beggar,
they will lay out ten to see a dead Indian. Legged like a
man! And his fins like arms! Warm, o' my troth! I do
now let loose my opinion, hold it no longer. This is no
fish, but an islander that hath lately suffered by a
thunderbolt.

Thunder

Alas, the storm is come again. My best way is to creep
under his gaberdine. There is no other shelter hereabout.
Misery acquaints a man with strange bed-fellows. I
40 will here shroud till the dregs of the storm be past.

Enter Stephano, singing, a bottle in his hand

STEPHANO

> I shall no more to sea, to sea,
> Here shall I die ashore.

This is a very scurvy tune to sing at a man's funeral.
Well, here's my comfort.

He drinks and then sings

> The master, the swabber, the boatswain, and I,
> The gunner and his mate,
> Loved Mall, Meg, and Marian, and Margery,

  But none of us cared for Kate.
  For she had a tongue with a tang,
  Would cry to a sailor, 'Go hang!'   50
 She loved not the savour of tar nor of pitch,
 Yet a tailor might scratch her where'er she did itch.
  Then to sea, boys, and let her go hang!
This is a scurvy tune too. But here's my comfort.
  He drinks

CALIBAN Do not torment me! O!

STEPHANO What's the matter? Have we devils here? Do
you put tricks upon's with savages and men of Ind, ha?
I have not 'scaped drowning to be afeard now of your
four legs. For it hath been said, 'As proper a man as
ever went on four legs cannot make him give ground'; 60
and it shall be said so again, while Stephano breathes at'
nostrils.

CALIBAN The spirit torments me! O!

STEPHANO This is some monster of the isle with four
legs, who hath got, as I take it, an ague. Where the devil
should he learn our languáge? I will give him some
relief, if it be but for that. If I can recover him, and keep
him tame, and get to Naples with him, he's a present
for any emperor that ever trod on neat's leather.

CALIBAN Do not torment me, prithee. I'll bring my wood 70
home faster.

STEPHANO He's in his fit now, and does not talk after the
wisest. He shall taste of my bottle. If he have never
drunk wine afore, it will go near to remove his fit. If I
can recover him, and keep him tame, I will not take too
much for him. He shall pay for him that hath him, and
that soundly.

CALIBAN Thou dost me yet but little hurt. Thou wilt
anon. I know it by thy trembling. Now Prosper works
upon thee.   80

STEPHANO Come on your ways. Open your mouth. Here is that which will give language to you, cat. Open your mouth. This will shake your shaking, I can tell you, and that soundly. (*He gives Caliban wine*) You cannot tell who's your friend. Open your chaps again.

TRINCULO I should know that voice. It should be – but he is drowned, and these are devils. O, defend me!

STEPHANO Four legs and two voices – a most delicate monster. His forward voice now is to speak well of his friend. His backward voice is to utter foul speeches and to detract. If all the wine in my bottle will recover him, I will help his ague. Come! (*Caliban drinks*) Amen! I will pour some in thy other mouth.

TRINCULO Stephano!

STEPHANO Doth thy other mouth call me? Mercy, mercy! This is a devil, and no monster. I will leave him; I have no long spoon.

TRINCULO Stephano! If thou beest Stephano, touch me and speak to me; for I am Trinculo – be not afeard – thy good friend Trinculo.

STEPHANO If thou beest Trinculo, come forth. I'll pull thee by the lesser legs. If any be Trinculo's legs, these are they. Thou art very Trinculo indeed! How cam'st thou to be the siege of this mooncalf? Can he vent Trinculos?

TRINCULO I took him to be killed with a thunderstroke. But art thou not drowned, Stephano? I hope now thou art not drowned. Is the storm overblown? I hid me under the dead mooncalf's gaberdine for fear of the storm. And art thou living, Stephano? O Stephano, two Neapolitans 'scaped?

STEPHANO Prithee, do not turn me about. My stomach is not constant.

CALIBAN (*aside*)
These be fine things, an if they be not sprites.

That's a brave god, and bears celestial liquor.
I will kneel to him.

STEPHANO How didst thou 'scape? How cam'st thou
hither? Swear by this bottle how thou cam'st hither. I
escaped upon a butt of sack, which the sailors heaved
o'erboard, by this bottle, which I made of the bark of a 120
tree, with mine own hands, since I was cast ashore.

CALIBAN I'll swear upon that bottle to be thy true subject, for the liquor is not earthly.

STEPHANO Here! Swear, then, how thou escaped'st.

TRINCULO Swum ashore, man, like a duck. I can swim
like a duck, I'll be sworn.

STEPHANO Here, kiss the book. (*He gives him wine*)
Though thou canst swim like a duck, thou art made like
a goose.

TRINCULO O Stephano, hast any more of this? 130

STEPHANO The whole butt, man. My cellar is in a rock
by th'seaside, where my wine is hid. How now, mooncalf? How does thine ague?

CALIBAN Hast thou not dropped from heaven?

STEPHANO Out o'th'moon, I do assure thee. I was the
Man i'th'Moon when time was.

CALIBAN I have seen thee in her, and I do adore thee. My
mistress showed me thee, and thy dog, and thy bush.

STEPHANO Come, swear to that. Kiss the book. I will
furnish it anon with new contents. Swear! (*Caliban* 140
drinks)

TRINCULO By this good light, this is a very shallow
monster! I afeard of him? A very weak monster! The
Man i'th'Moon? A most poor credulous monster! –
Well drawn, monster, in good sooth!

CALIBAN I'll show thee every fertile inch o'th'island, and
I will kiss thy foot. I prithee, be my god.

TRINCULO By this light, a most perfidious and drunken
monster! When's god's asleep, he'll rob his bottle.

CALIBAN I'll kiss thy foot. I'll swear myself thy subject.
150 STEPHANO Come on then. Down, and swear!

TRINCULO I shall laugh myself to death at this puppy-
headed monster. A most scurvy monster! I could find in
my heart to beat him –

STEPHANO Come, kiss.

TRINCULO But that the poor monster's in drink. An
abominable monster!

CALIBAN
I'll show thee the best springs. I'll pluck thee berries.
I'll fish for thee, and get thee wood enough.
A plague upon the tyrant that I serve!
160 I'll bear him no more sticks, but follow thee,
Thou wondrous man.

TRINCULO A most ridiculous monster, to make a wonder
of a poor drunkard!

CALIBAN
I prithee, let me bring thee where crabs grow;
And I with my long nails will dig thee pignuts,
Show thee a jay's nest, and instruct thee how
To snare the nimble marmoset. I'll bring thee
To clust'ring filberts, and sometimes I'll get thee
Young scamels from the rock. Wilt thou go with me?

170 STEPHANO I prithee now, lead the way without any more
talking. – Trinculo, the King and all our company else
being drowned, we will inherit here. Here, bear my
bottle. Fellow Trinculo, we'll fill him by and by again.

Caliban sings drunkenly

CALIBAN Farewell, master! Farewell, farewell!

TRINCULO A howling monster! A drunken monster!

CALIBAN
   No more dams I'll make for fish,
    Nor fetch in firing
    At requiring,

Nor scrape trenchering, nor wash dish.
>Ban, Ban, Cacaliban   180
>Has a new master – get a new man!
Freedom, high–day! High–day, freedom! Freedom,
high–day, freedom!

STEPHANO O brave monster! Lead the way.   *Exeunt*

*

Enter Ferdinand, bearing a log   III.1
FERDINAND
There be some sports are painful, and their labour
Delight in them sets off. Some kinds of baseness
Are nobly undergone, and most poor matters
Point to rich ends. This my mean task
Would be as heavy to me as odious, but
The mistress which I serve quickens what's dead,
And makes my labours pleasures. O, she is
Ten times more gentle than her father's crabbed,
And he's composed of harshness. I must remove
Some thousands of these logs and pile them up,   10
Upon a sore injunction. My sweet mistress
Weeps when she sees me work, and says such baseness
Had never like executor. I forget;
But these sweet thoughts do even refresh my labours,
Most busy lest when I do it.
        Enter Miranda, and Prospero at a distance, unseen
MIRANDA   Alas, now pray you
Work not so hard. I would the lightning had
Burnt up those logs that you are enjoined to pile!
Pray, set it down and rest you. When this burns,
'Twill weep for having wearied you. My father
Is hard at study. Pray now, rest yourself.   20

He's safe for these three hours.

FERDINAND   O most dear mistress,
The sun will set before I shall discharge
What I must strive to do.

MIRANDA   If you'll sit down,
I'll bear your logs the while. Pray, give me that.
I'll carry it to the pile.

FERDINAND   No, precious creature.
I had rather crack my sinews, break my back,
Than you should such dishonour undergo,
While I sit lazy by.

MIRANDA   It would become me
As well as it does you; and I should do it
With much more ease; for my good will is to it,
And yours it is against.

PROSPERO (*aside*)   Poor worm, thou art infected.
This visitation shows it.

MIRANDA   You look wearily.

FERDINAND

No, noble mistress, 'tis fresh morning with me
When you are by at night. I do beseech you,
Chiefly that I might set it in my prayers,
What is your name?

MIRANDA   Miranda. O my father,
I have broke your hest to say so!

FERDINAND   Admired Miranda!
Indeed, the top of admiration, worth
What's dearest to the world. Full many a lady
I have eyed with best regard, and many a time
Th'harmony of their tongues hath into bondage
Brought my too diligent ear. For several virtues
Have I liked several women; never any
With so full soul but some defect in her
Did quarrel with the noblest grace she owed,

And put it to the foil. But you, O you,
So perfect and so peerless, are created
Of every creature's best.

MIRANDA   I do not know
One of my sex; no woman's face remember,
Save, from my glass, mine own. Nor have I seen   50
More that I may call men than you, good friend,
And my dear father. How features are abroad
I am skill-less of; but, by my modesty,
The jewel in my dower, I would not wish
Any companion in the world but you.
Nor can imagination form a shape,
Besides yourself, to like of. But I prattle
Something too wildly, and my father's precepts
I therein do forget.

FERDINAND   I am, in my condition,
A prince, Miranda; I do think, a king –   60
I would not so – and would no more endure
This wooden slavery than to suffer
The flesh-fly blow my mouth. Hear my soul speak.
The very instant that I saw you did
My heart fly to your service, there resides
To make me slave to it; and for your sake
Am I this patient log-man.

MIRANDA   Do you love me?

FERDINAND
O heaven, O earth, bear witness to this sound,
And crown what I profess with kind event,
If I speak true! If hollowly, invert   70
What best is boded me to mischief! I,
Beyond all limit of what else i'th'world,
Do love, prize, honour you.

MIRANDA   I am a fool
To weep at what I am glad of.

III.1

PROSPERO (*aside*)   Fair encounter
   Of two most rare affections. Heavens rain grace
   On that which breeds between 'em.

FERDINAND   Wherefore weep you?

MIRANDA
   At mine unworthiness, that dare not offer
   What I desire to give, and much less take
   What I shall die to want. But this is trifling;
80   And all the more it seeks to hide itself,
   The bigger bulk it shows. Hence, bashful cunning!
   And prompt me, plain and holy innocence.
   I am your wife, if you will marry me.
   If not, I'll die your maid. To be your fellow
   You may deny me, but I'll be your servant
   Whether you will or no.

FERDINAND   My mistress, dearest,
   And I thus humble ever.

MIRANDA   My husband, then?

FERDINAND
   Ay, with a heart as willing
   As bondage e'er of freedom. Here's my hand.

MIRANDA
90   And mine, with my heart in't; and now farewell
   Till half an hour hence.

FERDINAND   A thousand, thousand!

    Exeunt Ferdinand and Miranda in different directions

PROSPERO
   So glad of this as they I cannot be,
   Who are surprised with all, but my rejoicing
   At nothing can be more. I'll to my book,
   For yet ere suppertime must I perform
   Much business appertaining.   *Exit*

STEPHANO Tell not me! When the butt is out we will
drink water; not a drop before. Therefore, bear up and
board 'em. Servant monster, drink to me.

TRINCULO Servant monster? The folly of this island!
They say there's but five upon this isle. We are three of
them. If th'other two be brained like us, the state totters.

STEPHANO Drink, servant monster, when I bid thee.
Thy eyes are almost set in thy head.

TRINCULO Where should they be set else? He were a
brave monster indeed if they were set in his tail.   10

STEPHANO My man-monster hath drowned his tongue
in sack. For my part, the sea cannot drown me. I swam,
ere I could recover the shore, five and thirty leagues off
and on. By this light, thou shalt be my lieutenant,
monster, or my standard.

TRINCULO Your lieutenant, if you list; he's no standard.

STEPHANO We'll not run, Monsieur Monster.

TRINCULO Nor go neither; but you'll lie like dogs, and
yet say nothing neither.

STEPHANO Mooncalf, speak once in thy life, if thou beest   20
a good mooncalf.

CALIBAN
How does thy honour? Let me lick thy shoe.
I'll not serve him: he is not valiant.

TRINCULO Thou liest, most ignorant monster! I am in
case to justle a constable. Why, thou deboshed fish,
thou, was there ever man a coward that hath drunk so
much sack as I today? Wilt thou tell a monstrous lie,
being but half a fish and half a monster?

CALIBAN Lo, how he mocks me! Wilt thou let him, my
lord?   30

TRINCULO 'Lord', quoth he? That a monster should be
such a natural!

CALIBAN Lo, lo, again! Bite him to death, I prithee.

STEPHANO Trinculo, keep a good tongue in your head.
If you prove a mutineer – the next tree! The poor
monster's my subject, and he shall not suffer indignity.

CALIBAN I thank my noble lord. Wilt thou be pleased to
hearken once again to the suit I made to thee?

STEPHANO Marry, will I. Kneel, and repeat it. I will
40 stand, and so shall Trinculo.

Enter Ariel, invisible

CALIBAN As I told thee before, I am subject to a tyrant,
a sorcerer, that by his cunning hath cheated me of the
island.

ARIEL Thou liest.

CALIBAN (*to Trinculo*)
Thou liest, thou jesting monkey, thou.
I would my valiant master would destroy thee!
I do not lie.

STEPHANO Trinculo, if you trouble him any more in's
tale, by this hand, I will supplant some of your teeth.

50 TRINCULO Why, I said nothing.

STEPHANO Mum, then, and no more. Proceed!

CALIBAN
I say, by sorcery he got this isle;
From me he got it. If thy greatness will
Revenge it on him – for I know thou dar'st,
But this thing dare not –

STEPHANO That's most certain.

CALIBAN
Thou shalt be lord of it, and I'll serve thee.

STEPHANO How now shall this be compassed? Canst
thou bring me to the party?

CALIBAN
60 Yea, yea, my lord, I'll yield him thee asleep,
Where thou mayst knock a nail into his head.

ARIEL Thou liest, thou canst not.

CALIBAN
   What a pied ninny's this! Thou scurvy patch!
   I do beseech thy greatness give him blows,
   And take his bottle from him. When that's gone,
   He shall drink naught but brine, for I'll not show him
   Where the quick freshes are.

STEPHANO Trinculo, run into no further danger. Inter-
   rupt the monster one word further and, by this hand,
   I'll turn my mercy out o'doors, and make a stockfish of 70
   thee.

TRINCULO Why, what did I? I did nothing. I'll go
   farther off.

STEPHANO Didst thou not say he lied?

ARIEL Thou liest.

STEPHANO Do I so? Take thou that!
   He strikes Trinculo
   As you like this, give me the lie another time.

TRINCULO I did not give the lie. Out o'your wits, and
   hearing too? A pox o' your bottle! This can sack and
   drinking do. A murrain on your monster, and the devil 80
   take your fingers!

CALIBAN Ha, ha, ha!

STEPHANO Now forward with your tale. – Prithee, stand
   further off.

CALIBAN
   Beat him enough. After a little time,
   I'll beat him too.

STEPHANO Stand farther. – Come, proceed.

CALIBAN
   Why, as I told thee, 'tis a custom with him
   I'th'afternoon to sleep. There thou mayst brain him,
   Having first seized his books; or with a log   90
   Batter his skull, or paunch him with a stake,
   Or cut his weasand with thy knife. Remember
   First to possess his books, for without them

He's but a sot, as I am, nor hath not
One spirit to command. They all do hate him
As rootedly as I. Burn but his books.
He has brave utensils, for so he calls them,
Which, when he has a house, he'll deck withal.
And that most deeply to consider is
100   The beauty of his daughter. He himself
Calls her a nonpareil. I never saw a woman
But only Sycorax my dam and she;
But she as far surpasseth Sycorax
As great'st does least.

STEPHANO   Is it so brave a lass?

CALIBAN

Ay, lord. She will become thy bed, I warrant,
And bring thee forth brave brood.

STEPHANO Monster, I will kill this man. His daughter
and I will be King and Queen – save our graces! – and
Trinculo and thyself shall be viceroys. Dost thou like
110   the plot, Trinculo?

TRINCULO Excellent.

STEPHANO Give me thy hand. I am sorry I beat thee;
but, while thou livest, keep a good tongue in thy head.

CALIBAN

Within this half hour will he be asleep.
Wilt thou destroy him then?

STEPHANO   Ay, on mine honour.

ARIEL This will I tell my master.

CALIBAN

Thou mak'st me merry. I am full of pleasure.
Let us be jocund! Will you troll the catch
You taught me but while-ere?

120 STEPHANO At thy request, monster, I will do reason, any
reason. Come on, Trinculo, let us sing.

    Sings

        Flout 'em and scout 'em,

And scout 'em and flout 'em!
Thought is free.

CALIBAN That's not the tune.

Ariel plays the tune on a tabor and pipe

STEPHANO What is this same?

TRINCULO This is the tune of our catch, played by the picture of Nobody.

STEPHANO If thou beest a man, show thyself in thy likeness. If thou beest a devil, take't as thou list.   130

TRINCULO O, forgive me my sins!

STEPHANO He that dies pays all debts. I defy thee. Mercy upon us!

CALIBAN Art thou afeard?

STEPHANO No, monster, not I.

CALIBAN
Be not afeard; the isle is full of noises,
Sounds, and sweet airs, that give delight and hurt not.
Sometimes a thousand twangling instruments
Will hum about mine ears; and sometime voices
That, if I then had waked after long sleep,   140
Will make me sleep again; and then, in dreaming,
The clouds methought would open, and show riches
Ready to drop upon me, that when I waked
I cried to dream again.

STEPHANO This will prove a brave kingdom to me, where I shall have my music for nothing.

CALIBAN When Prospero is destroyed.

STEPHANO That shall be by and by. I remember the story.

TRINCULO The sound is going away. Let's follow it, and   150
after do our work.

STEPHANO Lead, monster; we'll follow. I would I could see this taborer! He lays it on.

TRINCULO Wilt come? – I'll follow, Stephano.

Exeunt

III.3   *Enter Alonso, Sebastian, Antonio, Gonzalo, Adrian,*
        Francisco, and others

GONZALO

By 'r lakin, I can go no further, sir.
My old bones aches. Here's a maze trod indeed,
Through forthrights and meanders! By your patience,
I needs must rest me.

ALONSO

                 Old lord, I cannot blame thee,
Who am myself attached with weariness
To th'dulling of my spirits. Sit down and rest.
Even here I will put off my hope, and keep it
No longer for my flatterer. He is drowned

10   Whom thus we stray to find, and the sea mocks
Our frustrate search on land. Well, let him go.

ANTONIO (*aside to Sebastian*)

I am right glad that he's so out of hope.
Do not, for one repulse, forgo the purpose
That you resolved t'effect.

SEBASTIAN (*aside to Antonio*)

                   The next advantage
Will we take throughly.

ANTONIO   Let it be tonight;
For, now they are oppressed with travel, they
Will not, nor cannot, use such vigilance
As when they are fresh.

SEBASTIAN (*aside to Antonio*)

              I say tonight. No more.

Solemn and strange music; and Prospero on the top,
invisible. Enter several strange shapes, bringing in a
banquet; and dance about it with gentle actions of salu-
tations; and, inviting the King, etc., to eat, they depart

ALONSO

What harmony is this? My good friends, hark!

GONZALO Marvellous sweet music!

ALONSO
  Give us kind keepers, heavens! What were these?

SEBASTIAN
  A living drollery. Now I will believe
  That there are unicorns; that in Arabia
  There is one tree, the phoenix' throne, one phoenix
  At this hour reigning there.

ANTONIO   I'll believe both;
  And what does else want credit, come to me
  And I'll be sworn 'tis true. Travellers ne'er did lie,
  Though fools at home condemn 'em.

GONZALO   If in Naples
  I should report this now, would they believe me?
  If I should say I saw such islanders? –
  For certes, these are people of the island –
  Who, though they are of monstrous shape, yet note,
  Their manners are more gentle, kind, than of
  Our human generation you shall find
  Many, nay, almost any.

PROSPERO (aside)   Honest lord,
  Thou hast said well, for some of you there present
  Are worse than devils.

ALONSO   I cannot too much muse
  Such shapes, such gesture, and such sound, expressing,
  Although they want the use of tongue, a kind
  Of excellent dumb discourse.

PROSPERO (aside)   Praise in departing.

FRANCISCO
  They vanished strangely.

SEBASTIAN   No matter, since
  They have left their viands behind, for we have
        stomachs.
  Will't please you taste of what is here?

ALONSO   Not I.

GONZALO

Faith, sir, you need not fear. When we were boys,
Who would believe that there were mountaineers
Dewlapped like bulls, whose throats had hanging at 'em
Wallets of flesh? Or that there were such men
Whose heads stood in their breasts? Which now we find
Each putter-out of five for one will bring us
50   Good warrant of.

ALONSO   I will stand to and feed,
Although my last – no matter, since I feel
The best is past. Brother, my lord the Duke,
Stand to, and do as we.

> *Thunder and lightning. Enter Ariel, like a harpy,*
> *claps his wings upon the table, and, with a quaint*
> *device, the banquet vanishes*

ARIEL

You are three men of sin, whom destiny –
That hath to instrument this lower world
And what is in't – the never-surfeited sea
Hath caused to belch up you, and on this island
Where man doth not inhabit, you 'mongst men
Being most unfit to live. I have made you mad;
60   And even with suchlike valour men hang and drown
Their proper selves.

> *Alonso, Sebastian, and the others draw their swords*
>   You fools! I and my fellows
Are ministers of Fate. The elements,
Of whom your swords are tempered, may as well
Wound the loud winds, or with bemocked-at stabs
Kill the still-closing waters, as diminish
One dowle that's in my plume. My fellow ministers
Are like invulnerable. If you could hurt,
Your swords are now too massy for your strengths,

And will not be uplifted. But remember –
For that's my business to you – that you three   70
From Milan did supplant good Prospero,
Exposed unto the sea, which hath requit it,
Him and his innocent child; for which foul deed
The powers, delaying, not forgetting, have
Incensed the seas and shores, yea, all the creatures
Against your peace. Thee of thy son, Alonso,
They have bereft; and do pronounce by me
Lingering perdition – worse than any death
Can be at once – shall step by step attend
You and your ways; whose wraths to guard you from,   80
Which here, in this most desolate isle, else falls
Upon your heads, is nothing but heart's sorrow,
And a clear life ensuing.

> *He vanishes in thunder. Then, to soft music, enter the*
> *shapes again, and dance with mocks and mows, carry-*
> *ing out the table*

PROSPERO
Bravely the figure of this harpy hast thou
Performed, my Ariel: a grace it had, devouring.
Of my instruction hast thou nothing bated
In what thou hadst to say. So, with good life
And observation strange, my meaner ministers
Their several kinds have done. My high charms work,
And these, mine enemies, are all knit up   90
In their distractions. They now are in my power;
And in these fits I leave them while I visit
Young Ferdinand, whom they suppose is drowned,
And his and mine loved darling.

Exit

GONZALO
I'th'name of something holy, sir, why stand you
In this strange stare?

ALONSO

O, it is monstrous, monstrous!
Methought the billows spoke, and told me of it;
The winds did sing it to me; and the thunder,
100   That deep and dreadful organ-pipe, pronounced
The name of Prosper: it did bass my trespass.
Therefore my son i'th'ooze is bedded, and
I'll seek him deeper than e'er plummet sounded,
And with him there lie mudded.   *Exit*

SEBASTIAN   But one fiend at a time,
I'll fight their legions o'er.

ANTONIO   I'll be thy second.
               Exeunt Antonio and Sebastian

GONZALO

All three of them are desperate. Their great guilt,
Like poison given to work a great time after,
Now 'gins to bite the spirits. I do beseech you,
That are of suppler joints, follow them swiftly,
110   And hinder them from what this ecstasy
May now provoke them to.

ADRIAN   Follow, I pray you.
                     Exeunt

*

IV.1   *Enter Prospero, Ferdinand, and Miranda*

PROSPERO

If I have too austerely punished you,
Your compensation makes amends, for I
Have given you here a third of mine own life,
Or that for which I live; who once again
I tender to thy hand. All thy vexations
Were but my trials of thy love, and thou

Hast strangely stood the test. Here, afore heaven,
I ratify this my rich gift. O Ferdinand,
Do not smile at me that I boast her off,
For thou shalt find she will outstrip all praise,   10
And make it halt behind her.

FERDINAND   I do believe it
Against an oracle.

PROSPERO
Then, as my gift, and thine own acquisition
Worthily purchased, take my daughter; but
If thou dost break her virgin-knot before
All sanctimonious ceremonies may
With full and holy rite be ministered,
No sweet aspersion shall the heavens let fall
To make this contract grow; but barren hate,
Sour-eyed disdain and discord shall bestrew   20
The union of your bed with weeds so loathly
That you shall hate it both. Therefore take heed,
As Hymen's lamps shall light you.

FERDINAND   As I hope
For quiet days, fair issue, and long life,
With such love as 'tis now, the murkiest den,
The most opportune place, the strong'st suggestion
Our worser genius can, shall never melt
Mine honour into lust, to take away
The edge of that day's celebration
When I shall think or Phoebus' steeds are foundered   30
Or Night kept chained below.

PROSPERO   Fairly spoke.
Sit then and talk with her: she is thine own.
What, Ariel! My industrious servant, Ariel!
        Enter Ariel

ARIEL
What would my potent master? Here I am.

PROSPERO

Thou and thy meaner fellows your last service
Did worthily perform, and I must use you
In such another trick. Go bring the rabble,
O'er whom I give thee power, here to this place.
Incite them to quick motion, for I must
40   Bestow upon the eyes of this young couple
Some vanity of mine art. It is my promise,
And they expect it from me.

ARIEL   Presently?

PROSPERO

Ay, with a twink.

ARIEL

Before you can say 'Come' and 'Go',
And breathe twice, and cry, 'So, So',
Each one, tripping on his toe,
Will be here with mop and mow.
Do you love me, master? No?

PROSPERO

Dearly, my delicate Ariel. Do not approach
50   Till thou dost hear me call.

ARIEL   Well, I conceive.   *Exit*

PROSPERO

Look thou be true. Do not give dalliance
Too much the rein. The strongest oaths are straw
To th'fire i'th'blood. Be more abstemious,
Or else, good night your vow.

FERDINAND   I warrant you, sir,
The white cold virgin snow upon my heart
Abates the ardour of my liver.

PROSPERO   Well.
Now come, my Ariel! Bring a corollary,
Rather than want a spirit. Appear, and pertly.
No tongue! All eyes! Be silent.

Soft music. Enter Iris

IRIS

Ceres, most bounteous lady, thy rich leas   60
Of wheat, rye, barley, fetches, oats, and pease;
Thy turfy mountains, where live nibbling sheep,
And flat meads thatched with stover, them to keep;
Thy banks with pionèd and twillèd brims,
Which spongy April at thy hest betrims,
To make cold nymphs chaste crowns; and thy broom-
    groves,
Whose shadow the dismissèd bachelor loves,
Being lass-lorn: thy pole-clipt vineyard,
And thy sea-marge, sterile and rocky-hard,
Where thou thyself dost air – the queen o'th'sky,   70
Whose wat'ry arch and messenger am I,
Bids thee leave these, and with her sovereign grace
Here on this grass-plot, in this very place,
To come and sport. Her peacocks fly amain.
   Juno descends
Approach, rich Ceres, her to entertain.
   Enter Ceres

CERES

Hail, many-coloured messenger, that ne'er
Dost disobey the wife of Jupiter;
Who, with thy saffron wings, upon my flowers
Diffusest honey-drops, refreshing showers;
And with each end of thy blue bow dost crown   80
My bosky acres and my unshrubbed down,
Rich scarf to my proud earth. Why hath thy queen
Summoned me hither to this short-grassed green?

IRIS

A contract of true love to celebrate,
And some donation freely to estate
On the blest lovers.

IV.1

CERES   Tell me, heavenly bow,
If Venus or her son, as thou dost know,
Do now attend the queen? Since they did plot
The means that dusky Dis my daughter got,
90   Her and her blind boy's scandalled company
I have forsworn.

IRIS   Of her society
Be not afraid. I met her deity
Cutting the clouds towards Paphos, and her son
Dove-drawn with her. Here thought they to have done
Some wanton charm upon this man and maid,
Whose vows are, that no bed-right shall be paid
Till Hymen's torch be lighted: but in vain.
Mars's hot minion is returned again;
Her waspish-headed son has broke his arrows,
100   Swears he will shoot no more, but play with sparrows,
And be a boy right out.

CERES   Highest queen of state,
Great Juno comes; I know her by her gait.

JUNO
How does my bounteous sister? Go with me
To bless this twain, that they may prosperous be,
And honoured in their issue.
             They sing

JUNO
        Honour, riches, marriage blessing,
        Long continuance, and increasing,
        Hourly joys be still upon you!
        Juno sings her blessings on you.

CERES
110   Earth's increase, foison plenty,
        Barns and garners never empty,
        Vines with clust'ring bunches growing,
        Plants with goodly burden bowing;

118

Spring come to you at the farthest
In the very end of harvest.
Scarcity and want shall shun you,
Ceres' blessing so is on you.

FERDINAND
This is a most majestic vision, and
Harmonious charmingly. May I be bold
To think these spirits?

PROSPERO   Spirits, which by mine art   120
I have from their confines called to enact
My present fancies.

FERDINAND   Let me live here ever!
So rare a wondered father and a wise
Makes this place Paradise.

Juno and Ceres whisper, and send Iris on employment

PROSPERO   Sweet, now, silence!
Juno and Ceres whisper seriously.
There's something else to do. Hush and be mute,
Or else our spell is marred.

IRIS
You nymphs, called Naiades, of the windring brooks,
With your sedged crowns and ever-harmless looks,
Leave your crisp channels, and on this green land   130
Answer your summons; Juno does command.
Come temperate nymphs, and help to celebrate
A contract of true love. Be not too late.

Enter certain Nymphs

You sunburned sicklemen, of August weary,
Come hither from the furrow, and be merry.
Make holiday; your rye-straw hats put on,
And these fresh nymphs encounter every one
In country footing.

*Enter certain Reapers, properly habited. They join
with the Nymphs in a graceful dance, towards the end*

whereof, Prospero starts suddenly and speaks; after
which, to a strange, hollow, and confused noise, they
heavily vanish

PROSPERO (*aside*)
I had forgot that foul conspiracy
140 Of the beast Caliban and his confederates
Against my life. The minute of their plot
Is almost come. – Well done! Avoid! No more! –

FERDINAND
This is strange. Your father's in some passion
That works him strongly.

MIRANDA   Never till this day
Saw I him touched with anger so distempered.

PROSPERO
You do look, my son, in a moved sort,
As if you were dismayed. Be cheerful, sir.
Our revels now are ended. These our actors,
As I foretold you, were all spirits, and
150 Are melted into air, into thin air;
And, like the baseless fabric of this vision,
The cloud-capped towers, the gorgeous palaces,
The solemn temples, the great globe itself,
Yea, all which it inherit, shall dissolve,
And, like this insubstantial pageant faded,
Leave not a rack behind. We are such stuff
As dreams are made on; and our little life
Is rounded with a sleep. Sir, I am vext.
Bear with my weakness; my old brain is troubled.
160 Be not disturbed with my infirmity.
If you be pleased, retire into my cell
And there repose. A turn or two I'll walk,
To still my beating mind.

FERDINAND *and* MIRANDA We wish your peace.
                    Exeunt Ferdinand and Miranda

PROSPERO
Come with a thought. I thank thee, Ariel. Come!
Enter Ariel

ARIEL
Thy thoughts I cleave to. What's thy pleasure?

PROSPERO Spirit,
We must prepare to meet with Caliban.

ARIEL
Ay, my commander. When I presented Ceres,
I thought to have told thee of it, but I feared
Lest I might anger thee.

PROSPERO
Say again, where didst thou leave these varlets? 170

ARIEL
I told you, sir, they were red-hot with drinking.
So full of valour that they smote the air
For breathing in their faces, beat the ground
For kissing of their feet; yet always bending
Towards their project. Then I beat my tabor,
At which, like unbacked colts, they pricked their ears,
Advanced their eyelids, lifted up their noses
As they smelt music. So I charmed their ears
That calf-like they my lowing followed, through
Toothed briars, sharp furzes, pricking goss, and thorns, 180
Which entered their frail shins. At last I left them
I'th'filthy mantled pool beyond your cell,
There dancing up to th'chins, that the foul lake
O'erstunk their feet.

PROSPERO This was well done, my bird!
Thy shape invisible retain thou still.
The trumpery in my house, go bring it hither,
For stale to catch these thieves.

ARIEL I go, I go!
Exit

PROSPERO

> A devil, a born devil, on whose nature
> Nurture can never stick; on whom my pains,
190 Humanely taken, all, all lost, quite lost.
> And as with age his body uglier grows,
> So his mind cankers. I will plague them all
> Even to roaring.
>> *Enter Ariel, loaden with glistering apparel, etc.*
>> Come, hang them on this line.
>> *Enter Caliban, Stephano, and Trinculo, all wet*

CALIBAN

> Pray you, tread softly, that the blind mole may not
> Hear a foot fall. We now are near his cell.

STEPHANO Monster, your fairy, which you say is a harmless fairy, has done little better than played the Jack with us.

TRINCULO Monster, I do smell all horse-piss, at which 200 my nose is in great indignation.

STEPHANO So is mine. Do you hear, monster? If I should take a displeasure against you, look you –

TRINCULO Thou wert but a lost monster.

CALIBAN

> Good my lord, give me thy favour still.
> Be patient, for the prize I'll bring thee to
> Shall hoodwink this mischance. Therefore, speak softly.
> All's hushed as midnight yet.

TRINCULO Ay, but to lose our bottles in the pool –

STEPHANO There is not only disgrace and dishonour in 210 that, monster, but an infinite loss.

TRINCULO That's more to me than my wetting. Yet this is your harmless fairy, monster.

STEPHANO I will fetch off my bottle, though I be o'er ears for my labour.

CALIBAN

> Prithee, my king, be quiet. Seest thou here,

This is the mouth o'th'cell. No noise, and enter.
Do that good mischief which may make this island
Thine own for ever, and I, thy Caliban,
For aye thy foot-licker.

STEPHANO Give me thy hand. I do begin to have bloody 220
thoughts.

TRINCULO O King Stephano! O peer! O worthy
Stephano, look what a wardrobe here is for thee!

CALIBAN
Let it alone, thou fool! It is but trash.

TRINCULO O ho, monster! We know what belongs to a
frippery. O King Stephano!

STEPHANO Put off that gown, Trinculo. By this hand,
I'll have that gown!

TRINCULO Thy grace shall have it.

CALIBAN
The dropsy drown this fool! What do you mean   230
To dote thus on such luggage? Let't alone,
And do the murder first. If he awake,
From toe to crown he'll fill our skins with pinches,
Make us strange stuff.

STEPHANO Be you quiet, monster. Mistress line, is not
this my jerkin? Now is the jerkin under the line. Now,
jerkin, you are like to lose your hair and prove a bald
jerkin.

TRINCULO Do, do! We steal by line and level, an't like
your grace.   240

STEPHANO I thank thee for that jest. Here's a garment
for't. Wit shall not go unrewarded while I am king of
this country. 'Steal by line and level' is an excellent
pass of pate. There's another garment for't.

TRINCULO Monster, come put some lime upon your
fingers, and away with the rest.

CALIBAN
I will have none on't. We shall lose our time,

And all be turned to barnacles, or to apes
With foreheads villainous low.

250 STEPHANO Monster, lay to your fingers. Help to bear
this away where my hogshead of wine is, or I'll turn you
out of my kingdom. Go to, carry this!

TRINCULO And this.

STEPHANO Ay, and this.

*A noise of hunters heard. Enter divers Spirits in shape
of dogs and hounds, hunting them about, Prospero and
Ariel setting them on*

PROSPERO Hey, Mountain, hey!

ARIEL Silver! There it goes, Silver!

PROSPERO Fury, Fury! There, Tyrant, there! Hark,
hark!

Caliban, Stephano, and Trinculo are driven out
Go, charge my goblins that they grind their joints
260 With dry convulsions, shorten up their sinews
With aged cramps, and more pinch-spotted make them
Than pard or cat o'mountain.

ARIEL   Hark, they roar!

PROSPERO
Let them be hunted soundly. At this hour
Lies at my mercy all mine enemies.
Shortly shall all my labours end, and thou
Shalt have the air at freedom. For a little
Follow, and do me service.   *Exeunt*

*

V.1   *Enter Prospero, in his magic robes, and Ariel*
PROSPERO
Now does my project gather to a head.
My charms crack not, my spirits obey, and time

Goes upright with his carriage. How's the day?

ARIEL

On the sixth hour, at which time, my lord,
You said our work should cease.

PROSPERO   I did say so,
When first I raised the tempest. Say, my spirit,
How fares the King and's followers?

ARIEL   Confined together
In the same fashion as you gave in charge,
Just as you left them – all prisoners, sir,
In the line-grove which weather-fends your cell.   10
They cannot budge till your release. The King,
His brother, and yours, abide all three distracted,
And the remainder mourning over them,
Brimful of sorrow and dismay; but chiefly,
Him that you termed, sir, the good old lord Gonzalo,
His tears runs down his beard like winter's drops
From eaves of reeds. Your charm so strongly works 'em
That if you now beheld them your affections
Would become tender.

PROSPERO   Dost thou think so, spirit?

ARIEL

Mine would, sir, were I human.

PROSPERO   And mine shall.   20
Hast thou, which art but air, a touch, a feeling
Of their afflictions, and shall not myself,
One of their kind, that relish all as sharply
Passion as they, be kindlier moved than thou art?
Though with their high wrongs I am struck to th'quick
Yet with my nobler reason 'gainst my fury
Do I take part. The rarer action is
In virtue than in vengeance. They being penitent,
The sole drift of my purpose doth extend
Not a frown further. Go release them, Ariel.   30

125

My charms I'll break, their senses I'll restore,
And they shall be themselves.

ARIEL   I'll fetch them, sir.

Exit

PROSPERO
Ye elves of hills, brooks, standing lakes, and groves,
And ye that on the sands with printless foot
Do chase the ebbing Neptune, and do fly him
When he comes back; you demi-puppets that
By moonshine do the green, sour ringlets make,
Whereof the ewe not bites; and you whose pastime
Is to make midnight mushrumps, that rejoice
40   To hear the solemn curfew, by whose aid –
Weak masters though ye be – I have bedimmed
The noontide sun, called forth the mutinous winds,
And 'twixt the green sea and the azured vault
Set roaring war; to the dread rattling thunder
Have I given fire, and rifted Jove's stout oak
With his own bolt; the strong-based promontory
Have I made shake, and by the spurs plucked up
The pine and cedar; graves at my command
Have waked their sleepers, oped, and let 'em forth
50   By my so potent art. But this rough magic
I here abjure, and when I have required
Some heavenly music – which even now I do –
To work mine end upon their senses that
This airy charm is for, I'll break my staff,
Bury it certain fathoms in the earth,
And deeper than did ever plummet sound
I'll drown my book.

Solemn music
Here enters Ariel before; then Alonso with a frantic
gesture, attended by Gonzalo; Sebastian and Antonio
in like manner, attended by Adrian and Francisco.

They all enter the circle which Prospero had made,
and there stand charmed; which Prospero observing,
speaks

A solemn air, and the best comforter
To an unsettled fancy, cure thy brains,
Now useless, boiled within thy skull. There stand,   60
For you are spell-stopped.
Holy Gonzalo, honourable man,
Mine eyes, ev'n sociable to the show of thine,
Fall fellowly drops. The charm dissolves apace.
And as the morning steals upon the night,
Melting the darkness, so their rising senses
Begin to chase the ignorant fumes that mantle
Their clearer reason. O good Gonzalo,
My true preserver, and a loyal sir
To him thou follow'st, I will pay thy graces   70
Home both in word and deed. Most cruelly
Didst thou, Alonso, use me and my daughter.
Thy brother was a furtherer in the act.
Thou art pinched for't now, Sebastian. Flesh and blood,
You, brother mine, that entertained ambition,
Expelled remorse and nature, whom, with Sebastian –
Whose inward pinches therefore are most strong –
Would here have killed your king, I do forgive thee,
Unnatural though thou art. Their understanding
Begins to swell, and the approaching tide   80
Will shortly fill the reasonable shore
That now lies foul and muddy. Not one of them
That yet looks on me, or would know me. Ariel,
Fetch me the hat and rapier in my cell.
I will discase me, and myself present
As I was sometime Milan. Quickly, spirit!
Thou shalt ere long be free.
    Ariel sings and helps to attire him

ARIEL

> Where the bee sucks, there suck I,
> In a cowslip's bell I lie;
> There I couch when owls do cry.
> On the bat's back I do fly
> After summer merrily.
> Merrily, merrily shall I live now,
> Under the blossom that hangs on the bough.

PROSPERO

Why, that's my dainty Ariel! I shall miss thee,
But yet thou shalt have freedom – so, so, so.
To the King's ship, invisible as thou art!
There shalt thou find the mariners asleep
Under the hatches. The Master and the Boatswain
Being awake, enforce them to this place,
And presently, I prithee.

ARIEL

I drink the air before me, and return
Or ere your pulse twice beat.   *Exit*

GONZALO

All torment, trouble, wonder, and amazement
Inhabits here. Some heavenly power guide us
Out of this fearful country!

PROSPERO   Behold, sir King,
The wronged Duke of Milan, Prospero.
For more assurance that a living prince
Does now speak to thee, I embrace thy body,
And to thee and thy company I bid
A hearty welcome.

ALONSO   Whe'er thou beest he or no,
Or some enchanted trifle to abuse me,
As late I have been, I not know. Thy pulse
Beats as of flesh and blood; and, since I saw thee,
Th'affliction of my mind amends, with which

I fear a madness held me. This must crave –
An if this be at all – a most strange story.
Thy dukedom I resign, and do entreat
Thou pardon me my wrongs. But how should Prospero
Be living, and be here?

PROSPERO   First, noble friend,   120
Let me embrace thine age, whose honour cannot
Be measured or confined.

GONZALO   Whether this be
Or be not, I'll not swear.

PROSPERO   You do yet taste
Some subtleties o'th'isle, that will not let you
Believe things certain. Welcome, my friends all!
(aside to Sebastian and Antonio)
But you, my brace of lords, were I so minded,
I here could pluck his highness' frown upon you,
And justify you traitors. At this time
I will tell no tales.

SEBASTIAN (aside) The devil speaks in him.

PROSPERO   No.
For you, most wicked sir, whom to call brother   130
Would even infect my mouth, I do forgive
Thy rankest fault – all of them; and require
My dukedom of thee, which perforce, I know,
Thou must restore.

ALONSO   If thou beest Prospero,
Give us particulars of thy preservation;
How thou hast met us here, whom three hours since
Were wracked upon this shore; where I have lost –
How sharp the point of this remembrance is! –
My dear son Ferdinand.

PROSPERO   I am woe for't, sir.

ALONSO
Irreparable is the loss, and patience   140

Says it is past her cure.

PROSPERO   I rather think
You have not sought her help, of whose soft grace
For the like loss, I have her sovereign aid,
And rest myself content.

ALONSO   You the like loss?

PROSPERO

As great to me, as late, and supportable
To make the dear loss, have I means much weaker
Than you may call to comfort you, for I
Have lost my daughter.

ALONSO   A daughter?
O heavens, that they were living both in Naples,
150   The King and Queen there! That they were, I wish
Myself were mudded in that oozy bed
Where my son lies. When did you lose your daughter?

PROSPERO

In this last tempest. I perceive these lords
At this encounter do so much admire
That they devour their reason, and scarce think
Their eyes do offices of truth, their words
Are natural breath. But, howsoe'er you have
Been justled from your senses, know for certain
That I am Prospero, and that very Duke
160   Which was thrust forth of Milan, who most strangely
Upon this shore, where you were wracked, was landed
To be the lord on't. No more yet of this,
For 'tis a chronicle of day by day,
Not a relation for a breakfast, nor
Befitting this first meeting. Welcome, sir.
This cell's my court. Here have I few attendants,
And subjects none abroad. Pray you, look in.
My dukedom since you have given me again,
I will requite you with as good a thing,
170   At least bring forth a wonder to content ye

As much as me my dukedom.

Here Prospero discovers Ferdinand and Miranda,
playing at chess

MIRANDA
Sweet lord, you play me false.

FERDINAND   No, my dearest love,
I would not for the world.

MIRANDA
Yes, for a score of kingdoms you should wrangle,
And I would call it fair play.

ALONSO   If this prove
A vision of the island, one dear son
Shall I twice lose.

SEBASTIAN   A most high miracle.

FERDINAND
Though the seas threaten, they are merciful.
I have cursed them without cause.

He comes forward, and kneels

ALONSO   Now all the blessings
Of a glad father compass thee about!   180
Arise, and say how thou cam'st here.

MIRANDA   O, wonder!
How many goodly creatures are there here!
How beauteous mankind is! O brave new world,
That has such people in't!

PROSPERO   'Tis new to thee.

ALONSO
What is this maid with whom thou wast at play?
Your eld'st acquaintance cannot be three hours.
Is she the goddess that hath severed us,
And brought us thus together?

FERDINAND   Sir, she is mortal;
But by immortal Providence, she's mine.
I chose her when I could not ask my father   190
For his advice, nor thought I had one. She

131

Is daughter to this famous Duke of Milan,
Of whom so often I have heard renown,
But never saw before; of whom I have
Received a second life; and second father
This lady makes him to me.

ALONSO   I am hers.
But, O, how oddly will it sound that I
Must ask my child forgiveness!

PROSPERO   There, sir, stop.
Let us not burden our remembrances with
200 A heaviness that's gone.

GONZALO   I have inly wept,
Or should have spoke ere this. Look down, you gods,
And on this couple drop a blessèd crown!
For it is you that have chalked forth the way
Which brought us hither.

ALONSO   I say amen, Gonzalo.

GONZALO
Was Milan thrust from Milan that his issue
Should become kings of Naples? O, rejoice
Beyond a common joy, and set it down
With gold on lasting pillars. In one voyage
Did Claribel her husband find at Tunis,
210 And Ferdinand her brother found a wife
Where he himself was lost; Prospero his dukedom
In a poor isle, and all of us ourselves
When no man was his own.

ALONSO (*to Ferdinand and Miranda*)
                      Give me your hands.
Let grief and sorrow still embrace his heart
That doth not wish you joy.

GONZALO   Be it so! Amen.

> *Enter Ariel, with the Master and Boatswain amazedly*
> *following*

O look sir, look sir, here is more of us!

I prophesied, if a gallows were on land,
This fellow could not drown. Now, blasphemy,
That swear'st grace o'erboard, not an oath on shore?
Hast thou no mouth by land? What is the news?   220

BOATSWAIN

The best news is that we have safely found
Our King and company; the next, our ship –
Which, but three glasses since, we gave out split –
Is tight and yare and bravely rigged, as when
We first put out to sea.

ARIEL *(aside to Prospero)* Sir, all this service
Have I done since I went.

PROSPERO *(aside to Ariel)*   My tricksy spirit!

ALONSO

These are not natural events. They strengthen
From strange to stranger. Say, how came you hither?

BOATSWAIN

If I did think, sir, I were well awake,
I'd strive to tell you. We were dead of sleep   230
And – how we know not – all clapped under hatches,
Where, but even now, with strange and several noises
Of roaring, shrieking, howling, jingling chains,
And more diversity of sounds, all horrible,
We were awaked; straightway at liberty;
Where we, in all our trim, freshly beheld
Our royal, good, and gallant ship, our Master
Cap'ring to eye her. On a trice, so please you,
Even in a dream, were we divided from them,
And were brought moping hither.

ARIEL *(aside to Prospero)*   Was't well done?   240

PROSPERO *(aside to Ariel)*

Bravely, my diligence. Thou shalt be free.

ALONSO

This is as strange a maze as e'er men trod,
And there is in this business more than nature

    Was ever conduct of. Some oracle
    Must rectify our knowledge.

PROSPERO   Sir, my liege,
    Do not infest your mind with beating on
    The strangeness of this business. At picked leisure,
    Which shall be shortly, single I'll resolve you,
    Which to you shall seem probable, of every
250   These happened accidents. Till when, be cheerful,
    And think of each thing well. (*aside to Ariel*) Come
           hither, spirit.
    Set Caliban and his companions free.
    Untie the spell.   *Exit Ariel*
              How fares my gracious sir?
    There are yet missing of your company
    Some few odd lads that you remember not.

    Enter Ariel, driving in Caliban, Stephano, and Trin-
    culo in their stolen apparel

STEPHANO Every man shift for all the rest, and let no
man take care for himself, for all is but fortune. Coragio,
bully-monster, coragio!

TRINCULO If these be true spies which I wear in my head,
260 here's a goodly sight!

CALIBAN
    O Setebos, these be brave spirits indeed!
    How fine my master is! I am afraid
    He will chastise me.

SEBASTIAN   Ha, ha!
    What things are these, my lord Antonio?
    Will money buy 'em?

ANTONIO   Very like. One of them
    Is a plain fish, and no doubt marketable.

PROSPERO
    Mark but the badges of these men, my lords,
    Then say if they be true. This misshapen knave,

His mother was a witch, and one so strong
That could control the moon, make flows and ebbs,   270
And deal in her command without her power.
These three have robbed me, and this demi-devil –
For he's a bastard one – had plotted with them
To take my life. Two of these fellows you
Must know and own. This thing of darkness I
Acknowledge mine.

CALIBAN   I shall be pinched to death.

ALONSO
Is not this Stephano, my drunken butler?

SEBASTIAN
He is drunk now. Where had he wine?

ALONSO
And Trinculo is reeling ripe. Where should they
Find this grand liquor that hath gilded 'em?   280
How cam'st thou in this pickle?

TRINCULO I have been in such a pickle since I saw you
last that I fear me will never out of my bones. I shall
not fear fly-blowing.

SEBASTIAN Why, how now, Stephano?

STEPHANO O, touch me not! I am not Stephano, but a
cramp!

PROSPERO You'd be king o'th'isle, sirrah?

STEPHANO I should have been a sore one, then.

ALONSO
This is a strange thing as e'er I looked on.   290

PROSPERO
He is as disproportioned in his manners
As in his shape. – Go, sirrah, to my cell.
Take with you your companions. As you look
To have my pardon, trim it handsomely.

CALIBAN
Ay, that I will; and I'll be wise hereafter,

And seek for grace. What a thrice double ass
Was I to take this drunkard for a god,
And worship this dull fool!

PROSPERO   Go to. Away!

ALONSO

Hence, and bestow your luggage where you found it.

SEBASTIAN

300 Or stole it, rather.

Exeunt Caliban, Stephano, and Trinculo

PROSPERO

Sir, I invite your highness and your train
To my poor cell, where you shall take your rest
For this one night; which, part of it, I'll waste
With such discourse as, I not doubt, shall make it
Go quick away – the story of my life,
And the particular accidents gone by
Since I came to this isle. And in the morn,
I'll bring you to your ship, and so to Naples,
Where I have hope to see the nuptial

310 Of these our dear-beloved solemnized;
And thence retire me to my Milan, where
Every third thought shall be my grave.

ALONSO   I long
To hear the story of your life, which must
Take the ear strangely.

PROSPERO   I'll deliver all,
And promise you calm seas, auspicious gales,
And sail so expeditious, that shall catch
Your royal fleet far off. – My Ariel, chick,
That is thy charge. Then to the elements
Be free, and fare thou well. – Please you, draw near.

Exeunt

Spoken by Prospero
Now my charms are all o'erthrown,
And what strength I have's mine own,
Which is most faint. Now 'tis true
I must be here confined by you,
Or sent to Naples. Let me not,
Since I have my dukedom got
And pardoned the deceiver, dwell
In this bare island by your spell;
But release me from my bands
With the help of your good hands.   10
Gentle breath of yours my sails
Must fill, or else my project fails,
Which was to please. Now I want
Spirits to enforce, art to enchant;
And my ending is despair,
Unless I be relieved by prayer,
Which pierces so, that it assaults
Mercy itself, and frees all faults.
As you from crimes would pardoned be,
Let your indulgence set me free.   *Exit* 20

COMMENTARY

REFERENCES to plays by Shakespeare not yet available in the New Penguin Shakespeare are to Peter Alexander's edition of the *Complete Works*, London, 1951.

The setting
This is at first a ship at sea, and afterwards an uninhabited island; but the Folio (F) describes the setting merely as 'an vn-inhabited Island', passing over the first scene on board Alonso's ship.

.1   See the Introduction, pages 7–8, for a discussion of this scene.

3   *Good*. The Master is acknowledging the prompt appearance of the Boatswain, not expressing optimism about the situation of the ship.
     yarely briskly

4   (stage direction) *Enter Mariners*. There is no exit marked for them in the Folio between this point and line 49, when they re-enter as a group, crying 'All lost!' Probably there should be a continual coming and going of mariners across the stage and occasionally an accidental collision between one of them and a member of the court party, giving point to the Boatswain's concern that his passengers keep below and out of the way.

6   *Tend* attend

7–8   *Blow till . . . room enough*. The Boatswain invites the storm to do its worst, provided the ship has space to manoeuvre in.

8   (stage direction) *Enter Alonso, Sebastian, Antonio, Ferdinand, Gonzalo, and others*. Shakespeare could have found the names in Eden's *History of Travel* (1577).

10   *Play the men* act like men

13   *Do you not hear him?* The Boatswain means them to listen to the sound of the Master's whistle off stage, as he directs the sailors. In the slight pause between the question and his next sentence, however, the noise of the storm itself is necessarily more striking than anything else. It, in fact, is 'the Master' that they hear.

15   *good* good fellow

16–17   *cares . . . roarers*. The use of a singular verb with a plural subject is common in Shakespeare, and occurs several times in *The Tempest*. *Roarers* are violent waves, with a secondary association of 'bully' or 'roisterer' which serves to underline the social as well as purely physical disintegration of the courtiers' normal world. See Introduction, pages 7–8.

22   *work the peace of the present*. The Boatswain suggests, sarcastically, that Gonzalo should use his skill as a councillor to calm the present storm.

29–30   *no drowning-mark . . . gallows*. Gonzalo is alluding to the proverb, 'He that's born to be hanged need fear no drowning'.

32   *doth little advantage* is of small help

34–5   *Down with . . . main-course*. Although the topsail has already been lowered, the ship continues to drift towards the rocks. In this emergency, the Boatswain orders the topmast to be struck, and tries to keep the ship close to the wind and away from the shore under the mainsail.

36   *A plague*. The F dash after the word *plague* may indicate that the actor was allowed to improvise some profanity here that could not be printed. Sebastian later calls the Boatswain blasphemous (lines 40–41) and Gonzalo in Act V (lines 218–19) seems to retain a

memory of language stronger than anything in the actual text.

36-7 *They are louder than the weather, or our office.* The Boatswain complains that the passengers make more noise than the storm, drowning out the Master's whistle and his own commands.

47 *unstanched* loose

48 *Lay her a-hold* bring the ship close to the wind (so as to hold her steady)

Set her two courses (set the foresail in addition to the mainsail, so that the ship may move 'Off to sea again')

49 (stage direction) *Enter Mariners wet.* This direction underlines the realism of the opening scene.

51 *What, must our mouths be cold?* Elizabethan sailors were known to seek comfort in drink during moments of crisis and some editors have interpreted the Boatswain's words to mean that he has recourse to a pocket-flask at this point. Antonio, a few lines later (line 54), does talk about 'drunkards', but it is never easy to credit his abuse.

54 *merely* completely

55 *wide-chopped* wide-jawed

56 *ten tides.* Pirates were hanged on shore at the low-water mark and the bodies left there until three tides had washed over them. Antonio, who is in general prone to hyperbole, makes it ten in his disgust.

58 *glut* swallow

62 *heath* heather

furze gorse

I.2 See Introduction, pages 8–11, for a discussion of this scene.

(stage direction) *Enter Prospero and Miranda.* The fortunes of Prospero Adorno, Duke of Genoa, are related in Thomas's *History of Italy* (1549), and there is also a Prospero among the characters of Ben Jonson's

Every Man In His Humour (1598), a play in which Shakespeare himself acted. The name 'Miranda' seems to have been invented by Shakespeare.

4   *welkin's cheek* face of the sky

11   *or ere* before

13   *fraughting* forming the cargo of the ship

14   *piteous* pitying

20   *full* very

22   *meddle* mingle

23-5   *Lend thy hand . . . Lie there, my art.* Prospero has made use of his magic robe while raising the storm. Now, the first stage of his project successfully accomplished, he lays his supernatural power aside momentarily. Taking off his mantle, he sits down beside Miranda to describe his misfortunes before he became master of the island and its spirits. Not until this recital is ended does he stand up and (between lines 177 and 184) resume his robe in order to put Miranda to sleep and summon Ariel.

27   *virtue* essence

28   *provision* foresight

29-32   *that there is no soul . . . which thou sawst sink.* After starting out to assure Miranda that not a *soul* came to harm in the ship, Prospero changes his mind in mid-sentence. He greatly strengthens his claim, asserting that the people she laments have not lost so much as a *hair* in the disaster. Ariel later (I.2. 217) confirms this.

30   *perdition* loss

31   *Betid* happened

32   *Which thou heard'st . . . sawst sink.* The repeated relative pronoun *which* refers, strictly, to the creatures in the vessel the first time it is used, to the vessel itself the second. The effect, however, is to blur distinctions between the two, confounding passengers and ship, the articulate and the inarticulate, in a mutual chaos.

35   *bootless inquisition* fruitless questioning

41   *Out* fully

45-6   *an assurance | That my remembrance warrants* a certainty
guaranteed by memory

54   *Milan* (accent on the first syllable)

56   *piece* masterpiece

58-9   *heir | And princess* (sometimes emended to 'A princess'.
However, the F reading is clear enough: Prospero was
Duke of Milan, and his heir, the princess Miranda, of
equal nobility.)

59   *no worse issued* of no meaner descent

63   *holp* (past tense of 'help')

64-5   *teen that I have turned you to . . . my remembrance* grief
that I have made you remember by the necessity of
informing me about events I do not recall

66-74   *My brother and thy uncle . . . a parallel.* As he tries, for
the first time since coming to the island, to tell the
story of his exile from Milan, Prospero finds that he
wishes to say too many things at once. The subject
of Antonio's treachery is an especially painful one and,
as he approaches it, his narrative becomes more
emotional and less orderly. Beginning to describe
Antonio to Miranda, he suddenly remembers that he
has not yet told her as much as she ought to know
about Milan itself ('Through all the signories it was
the first . . .'). His sentence changes direction accordingly, and the relative clause ('he, whom next thyself')
in which Prospero starts to reveal the nature of
Antonio's crime is left incomplete and dangling. The
whole of Prospero's exposition here is worth comparing
with the infinitely smoother and more impersonal
narrative of old Egeon in the other play of Shakespeare's which observes the unities, *The Comedy of
Errors* (I.1.31-139).

69-70   *put | The manage of* entrusted the administration of

71   *signories* Italian states

78   *Dost thou attend me?* See Introduction, page 10, on
Prospero's concern over Miranda's inattention.

79   *perfected* fully skilled in

81   *To trash for over-topping.* The term *To trash* derives
       from hunting and means to check the speed of a hound
       which tends to out-run the pack by attaching a weight
       or cord to its neck. *Over-topping*, probably associated
       with gardening for most Elizabethans, means becoming
       excessive in size or importance. Characteristically,
       Prospero has compressed two distinct images here into
       one, describing Antonio's repression of ambitious
       elements in the state simultaneously in terms of speed
       and of height.

83   *key.* The initial meaning, derived from 'keys of office',
       transforms itself in the two succeeding lines into a
       musical image.

87   *verdure* vitality

90   *closeness* seclusion

91–2   *With that which ... all popular rate.* In themselves,
       Prospero's studies could not be over-valued. Yet by
       leading him to neglect the affairs of his dukedom they
       became dangerous, awakening the evil nature of
       Antonio.

94–6   *Like a good parent ... As my trust was.* Prospero is
       alluding to the common belief that an exceptional man
       is likely to produce an inferior or vicious son. His great
       trust in Antonio generated its opposite, a disloyalty as
       great as his own confidence.

97   *sans* without
       lorded made a lord of

98   *revenue* (accent on the second syllable)

100–105 *Who having into truth ... With all prerogative.* By
       continually telling a lie, one may come to believe in the
       fabrication oneself, thus committing a further sin
       against truth. This, Prospero suggests, is what
       happened to Antonio when he convinced himself that
       there was no difference between exercising the powers
       and enjoying the privileges of the Duke of Milan, lent
       him by his brother, and actually being the Duke.

100   *into* (with the sense of 'unto')

107–9   *To have no screen ... Absolute Milan.* Prospero describes Antonio as an actor, playing a royal part on the stage, who was determined to convert fiction into fact. To do so, he had to eliminate the division (*screen*) between the part he played and the reality it reflected, so that he might govern for his own benefit as absolute ruler of Milan and not for Prospero's.

108–16   *he needs will be ... ignoble stooping.* Here, as he comes to the events immediately responsible for his exile, Prospero momentarily abandons the past for the present tense. The effect (coupled with the tone of sarcasm introduced in lines 109–16) is to suggest how immediate and painful the memory still is.

112   *dry* thirsty

117   *his condition and th'event* his pact (with Naples) and its outcome

118–20   *I should sin ... bad sons.* Miranda varies Prospero's previous observation in lines 94–6.

123   *in lieu o'th'premises* in consideration of the pledge

125   *presently* immediately

131   *ministers for th'purpose* agents employed

132   *Me and thy crying self.* Coleridge said of this line: 'The power of poetry is, by a single word perhaps, to instil that energy into the mind which compels the imagination to produce the picture. Here by introducing a single happy epithet, "crying", a complete picture is presented to the mind, and in the production of such pictures the power of genius consists.' The compression characteristic of the play, its economy of utterance, certainly declares itself here. As Coleridge points out, the single word *crying* exacts visualization and expansion of what is given from the reader.

134   *hint* occasion

135   *wrings* forces

138   *impertinent* irrelevant

144   *In few* briefly

146   *butt* tub

148   *hoist* lifted up

149–51   *To cry to th'sea ... but loving wrong.* The deliberate artificiality of Prospero's language here, the abandonment of realism and probability in his description of this sea voyage, marks a new stage in the story. The ordinary world of Milan and Naples is separated by more than geographical space from this island. A voyage in which sea and winds are partners in lamentation, in which an infant not yet three years old remains uniformly cheerful, and an unseaworthy boat arrives at its destination without help from sail or mast, declares plainly that Prospero's island will not be found on any map.

155   *decked* covered (with a deliberately far-fetched sense of 'ornamented')

157   *undergoing stomach* spirit of endurance

159   *By Providence divine.* Miranda's question in the preceding line, 'How came we ashore?', is one which the audience may well want to ask too. Shakespeare allows it to be raised, but provides a deliberately vague and enigmatic answer. For the role of Providence in the play, see Introduction, pages 41–4.

165   *steaded* been of use

169   *Now I arise.* The words operate both as a concealed stage direction, indicating that at this point Prospero stands up and prepares to resume his magic robe, and as a general reference to the new development in his fortunes.

173   *Than other princess can* than other princesses can have

181   *zenith* high point of fortune

188   *Ariel.* Ariel is the name of an angel, or powerful spirit, in a variety of sources. Shakespeare, however, may well have arrived at the name without assistance.

193   *quality* companion spirits

194   *to point* in detail

196   *beak* prow

200   *boresprit* bowsprit

200 *distinctly* separately

207 *coil* tumult

209 *fever of the mad* fever such as madmen feel

213 *up-staring* standing on end

218 *sustaining*. In *Hamlet* (IV.7.176) Shakespeare had described Ophelia's garments as bearing her up, 'mermaid-like', for a while. The same fantasy presumably lies behind the use of the word *sustaining* here.

220 *In troops I have dispersed them 'bout the isle*. Ariel does not mention Stephano and Trinculo as composing one of these troops. On the question of whether they reached the island by accident, or because Prospero wished to use them to test Caliban, the play is silent.

224 *this sad knot*. Ariel imitates Ferdinand's position for Prospero's benefit.

229 *still-vexed Bermoothes* (the Bermudas, supposed to be continually (*still*) vexed by storms)

234 *flote* sea

239 *mid-season* noon

240 *two glasses*. The time is two o'clock.

242–300 *Is there more toil? . . . What shall I do?* Magicians always had some difficulty keeping the spirits who served them under control. Ariel's impatience to be free and Prospero's harsh and domineering attitude towards him in this scene must be explained, at least in part, with reference to this tradition.

250 *bate me* reduce my term of service

255 *veins o'th'earth* subterranean rivers

256 *baked* hardened

258 *Sycorax*. This name, which is not found outside *The Tempest*, is usually explained as a combination of the two Greek words *sys* (sow) and *korax* (raven).

261 *O, was she so!* Prospero's rejoinder is somewhat ambiguous. He may simply be agreeing sarcastically with Ariel, or he may be contradicting the notion that Sycorax was born in Argier (Algiers).

266–7 *For one thing she did . . . take her life*. Charles Lamb believed that Shakespeare was referring here to the story of the witch who saved Algiers in 1541 when it was besieged by Charles V. Most modern editors argue that Sycorax escaped death not for any good she had done, but simply because she was pregnant. Allusion to an unexplained incident in the past would, however, be entirely in keeping with the general practice of the play.

269 *blue-eyed.* A blue colour in the eye-lid was regarded as a sign of pregnancy.

272-4 *And for thou wast a spirit . . . she did confine thee.* The black magic of Sycorax was powerful enough to invoke a superior spirit like Ariel, but not to force him to obey her when summoned.

272 *for* because

274 *hests* commands

284 *Caliban.* The name seems to have been invented by Shakespeare. It has often been pointed out that *Caliban* is an anagram of 'cannibal'.

297-8 *I will be correspondent to command . . . gently* I will be responsive to command and execute my tasks graciously

301-3 *Go make thyself like a nymph o'th'sea . . . eyeball else.* Prospero may have thought that he would have occasion later to make Ariel visible to one or more members of the court party as a sea-nymph. The theatre audience benefits, in any case, from this 'invisible' disguise, and it is appropriate to the two songs Ariel sings to Ferdinand later in the Act.

311 *miss* do without

318 *Hark in thine ear.* This brief reappearance of Ariel as a sea-nymph not only permits Prospero (unheard by us) to instruct him to lead Ferdinand to his meeting with Miranda, but affords the audience an immediate and striking visual contrast between Ariel and Caliban, who enters immediately after.

319 *got by the devil himself.* Caliban is the product of an unholy union between a witch and a diabolic spirit.

326   *Urchins* spirits in the shape of hedgehogs

327   *for that vast of night that they may work* for that long
         period of darkness in which they are allowed to exercise
         their power

345   *stripes* lashes

351–62   *Abhorrèd slave ... more than a prison.* Many editions
         transfer this speech from Miranda to Prospero, on the
         grounds that its stern, argumentative tone is incom-
         patible with her character. But pity (line 353) is almost
         the keynote of Miranda's nature; she not infrequently
         echoes her father's style of speech (lines 117–19);
         Caliban later says that she has instructed him
         (II.2.137–8). In general, the distancing of characters in
         The Tempest makes it difficult to legislate about what
         may or may not be consistent with their over-all
         conception.

364   *red plague rid you* that form of plague which produces
         red sores destroy you

369   *old* such as old people have

370   *aches* (pronounced 'aitches')

373   *Setebos.* The name, Setebos, appears in Robert Eden's
         History of Travaile (1577) as that of a Patagonian god.
         Robert Browning, in 'Caliban Upon Setebos; or
         Natural Theology in the Island', explores the nature
         of this god as conceived of by Caliban.

377–8   *kissed | The wild waves whist.* The ordered measure of
         the dance stills the sea's violence. Precisely how this
         is brought about remains as vague as the syntax.

378   *whist* silent

379   *featly* nimbly

380   *And, sweet sprites, the burden bear.* The F arrangement
         of the song seems to have been dictated principally by
         the printer's convenience. It is unclear, as a result,
         precisely how much is sung by Ariel, and how much
         by the sprites who are enjoined to bear the burden, or
         refrain. The arrangement adopted here supposes that
         the sprites are responsible only for the scattered sounds

of watch-dogs barking, possibly for the distant crowing of cocks behind Ariel's reference in the concluding lines.

393   *passion* grief

397–403   *Full fathom five ... ring his knell.* The sea-change of which Ariel sings, the transmutation of the body of Ferdinand's father into substances 'rich and strange', makes this death suddenly unreal and without pain. It allows Ferdinand to turn his whole mind to Miranda, almost at once, without seeming callous or heedless of his loss.

406   *remember* recall

408   *owes* owns

409   *The fringèd curtains of thine eye advance.* Again, as in lines 149–58, the deliberate artificiality of the language guides our reactions. This will be a ritual, ceremonial first meeting of lovers.
        advance raise

420–21   *It goes on, I see, | As my soul prompts it.* Prospero can command Ariel to bring Ferdinand where Miranda is, can arrange a situation propitious to love at first sight. He cannot, however, compel them to fall in love.

423   *airs* (Ariel's music)

424   *remain* dwell

426   *bear* conduct

427   *O you wonder.* Ferdinand has, in fact, virtually anticipated Miranda's name.

428   *If you be maid or no* if you are mortal or a goddess

433   *single* (1) solitary; (2) helpless

434   *He does hear me.* Ferdinand believes himself to be King of Naples, his father being drowned. Therefore, in answer to Prospero's question (line 432), he asserts that he ('the best of them that speak this speech') and the King of Naples are now, unhappily, the same.

438–9   *the Duke of Milan | And his brave son being twain.* This is the only reference in the play to Antonio's son. Editors have used it to argue that the text of *The*

Tempest that we have was cut or revised, or else that Shakespeare was forgetful in his latter years. Antonio's son may, of course, be on his way back to Naples with the rest of the fleet (lines 232–7). It seems more likely, however, that he belongs to that deliberately suppressed portion of the play discussed in the Introduction, pages 14–17.

440   *control* refute

442   *changed eyes* fallen in love. Ferdinand is, in fact, so riveted by the sight of Miranda that Prospero has a good deal of trouble distracting his attention.

444   *you have done yourself some wrong.* Prospero is, of course, being heavily ironic.

458–60   *There's nothing ill can dwell ... will strive to dwell with't.* Miranda advances a conventional Neo-platonic idea in her defence of Ferdinand. His physical beauty must, she believes, reflect a noble nature – even as Caliban's ugliness expresses the deformity within.

466   *entertainment* treatment

469   *He's gentle, and not fearful* he is of noble birth and not a coward

470   *My foot my tutor?* does a dependent part of me, my daughter, presume to instruct me?

472   *ward* posture of defence

474–82   *Beseech you ... And they to him are angels.* Prospero may seem unnecessarily harsh with Miranda here. The severity of his attitude, however, has the effect of crystallizing her feelings with regard to Ferdinand and of dividing her from himself within a necessarily brief space of time.

482   *affections* inclinations

485   *nerves* sinews

496   *Hark what thou else shalt do me.* Prospero's unheard instructions to Ariel here presumably have something to do with the members of the court party excluding Ferdinand. The next time he appears, Ariel will be engaged in casting a charmed sleep over Alonso and

all his companions except Antonio and Sebastian. Prospero does not, however, allow the audience to partake of his plans, nor will it ever be possible to know exactly what his intentions were.

500   *then* till then

II.1   Coleridge remarked that in this scene Shakespeare showed 'the tendency in bad men to indulge in scorn and contemptuous expressions, as a mode of getting rid of their own uneasy feelings of inferiority to the good, and also, by making the good ridiculous, of rendering the transition of others to wickedness easy. Shakespeare never puts habitual scorn into the mouths of other than bad men.' The tendency of Antonio and Sebastian to drag the scene down into prose, as opposed to the verse of Alonso, Gonzalo, and Francisco, displays itself here at the very beginning and continues up to the point at which they begin to discuss their conspiracy.

3   *hint* occasion

5   *The masters of some merchant, and the merchant* the officers of some merchant vessel and her owner

9–11   *Prithee, peace . . . like cold porridge.* There is a pun here on 'peace' and 'pease', an ingredient of porridge.

12   *visitor* (parish visitor charged with comforting the sick and distressed)

17–107   *One : tell . . . daughter's marriage.* That Sebastian and Antonio do not mind being rude to Gonzalo to his face is evident from this interchange. Whether Gonzalo and the other nobles actually hear any of the subsequent mocks and jeers between this point and line 188 is a matter for the actors to decide. Antonio and Sebastian should, in any case, form a separate little enclave on the stage.

17   *One : tell* Gonzalo's wit has struck one – keep count

20   *A dollar.* Sebastian maliciously interprets Gonzalo's

152

word 'entertainer' to mean inn-keeper, giving a characteristically mercenary, prosaic meaning to what had been intended as a general caution against giving way to every grief that comes. Gonzalo's pun in the next line ('dolour') rescues his original meaning – to the annoyance of Sebastian.

38–9 *Ha, ha, ha . . . you're paid.* In the Folio, it is Sebastian who laughs and Antonio who remarks, 'So, you're paid'. However, it was Sebastian who wagered on Gonzalo ('the old cock') and lost the match when Adrian (the young 'cockerel') was the first to break silence. Accordingly, this edition reverses the Folio reading, giving Antonio, as winner of the bet, the laugh indicated.

45 *temperance* climate (taken by Antonio in the next line as a girl's name)

58 *eye* spot (or perhaps Gonzalo's optimistic eye)

68–9 *If but one of his pockets could speak, would it not say he lies?* Ariel (I.2.218–19) has already mentioned the fact that the garments of the shipwrecked nobles are fresher than before. They should appear so on the stage. The perceptions of Antonio and Sebastian are malevolently askew.

74 *'Twas a sweet marriage.* Sebastian is, of course, sarcastic.

78–87 *Not since widow Dido's time . . . I assure you, Carthage.* Dido was in fact the widow of Sychaeus at the time she met Aeneas, and Aeneas himself was a widower, having lost his wife Creusa on the night he fled from Troy. The homely terms 'widow' and 'widower', however, are scarcely appropriate to this story of tragic love. Antonio and Sebastian are quick to seize upon the absurdity of *widow Dido*, and to improve upon it, although at one point even Sebastian seems to find Antonio's hilarity excessive (line 82). The whole passage may well have held a meaning for Shakespeare's contemporaries that is lost to us.

153

88–9   *His word is more than the miraculous harp ... and houses too.* Only the walls of Thebes were raised by the sound of Amphion's harp. Gonzalo, by confusing Tunis with Carthage, has reared a whole new city, houses and all.

96–7   *Ay ... Why, in good time.* Either Gonzalo is, after a long pause for reflection, reaffirming his error about Tunis being Carthage or he turns again to Alonso, who *in good time* is beginning to take note of the conversation going on around him.

101   *And the rarest that e'er came there.* Antonio is mimicking Adrian's style of speech in lines 76–7.

102   *Bate* except

105   *in a sort* after a fashion

108–9 *You cram these words ... of my sense.* Alonso complains that Gonzalo forces him to hear words for which his mind has no appetite, that he is being force-fed.

111   *rate* opinion

115–24 *Sir, he may live ... alive to land.* Apart from three words in the banquet scene (III.3.41), this is Francisco's only speech in the play. Both he and Adrian are figures so shadowy and silent that it seems strange that Shakespeare should have troubled to give them names of their own. In *Cymbeline* and *The Winter's Tale*, characters with speaking parts considerably greater than Adrian's or Francisco's are designated merely as 'first' or 'second' gentleman. Again, the effect in *The Tempest* is to suggest the stripped-down and compressed.

122–3 *th'shore, that o'er his wave-worn ... to relieve him.* The image is of cliffs eroded by the surf at their base, and so seeming to bend over the sea compassionately.

129   *hath cause to wet the grief on't* have reason to weep over this lamentable situation

132–3 *Weighed between loathness and obedience ... should bow.* Claribel was torn between dislike of the African marriage and obedience to her father. The construction of the sentence is not entirely clear.

140   *And time to speak it in.* Gonzalo's loyalty to his sovereign does not extend to the point of defending the Tunisian marriage in itself, even as it did not let him, twelve years before, cast Prospero and his child adrift without provisions. It is the inhumanity of Sebastian in aggravating Alonso's griefs when they are most fresh which Gonzalo protests against, not what he actually says.

142   *chirugeonly* like a surgeon

145   *plantation.* Gonzalo means the word in the sense of colonization; Antonio wilfully misunderstands it as cultivation. These persistent mistakings of Gonzalo's meaning by the wicked lords, although deliberate, contribute to the general sense of failure of communication in the play.

150–67   *I'th'commonwealth ... my innocent people.* Gonzalo's ideal commonwealth is derived from a passage in Montaigne's essay 'Of Cannibals'. The whole essay is worth reading with relation to *The Tempest.* However, the specific verbal parallels are concentrated in one passage of Florio's translation of 1603:

'It is a nation ... that hath no kind of traffic, no knowledge of letters, no intelligence of numbers, no name of magistrate, nor of politic superiority; no use of service, of riches or of poverty; no contracts, no successions, no partitions, no occupation but idle; no respect of kindred, but common, no apparel but natural, no manuring of lands, no use of wine, corn, or metal. The very words that import lying, falsehood, treason, dissimulations, covetousness, envy, detraction, and pardon, were never heard of amongst them.'

150   *by contraries* contrary to usual practice

151   *traffic* business

153   *Letters* learning

154   *service* servants

             succession inheritance

155   *Bourn* limits of property

155   *tilth* agriculture

164   *engine* weapon

166   *it* its

       foison abundance

177   *minister occasion* provide opportunity (for wit)

178   *sensible* sensitive

184   *An* if

       flat-long (with the flat side of the sword, and therefore ineffective)

188   *bat-fowling* (using the moon as a lantern to attract birds, which could then be killed with sticks (bats))

190–91 *I will not adventure my discretion so weakly.* Gonzalo claims, in effect, that the sneers of Antonio and Sebastian are not worth a loss of temper.

197   *omit* disregard

211   *Th'occasion speaks thee* the moment itself speaks to you

220   *wink'st* keep your eyes shut

225   *Trebles thee o'er* makes you three times greater than you are at present

228–32 *If you but knew ... their own fear, or sloth.* Antonio appears to be suggesting that Sebastian's self-deprecatory tone in itself argues his need to cast off sloth and remove the impediments between himself and greatness.

233   *setting* fixed look

234   *matter* matter of importance

235   *throes thee much to yield* costs you much pain to bring forth

236–8 *Although this lord of weak remembrance.* Antonio begins with an unflattering reference to Gonzalo's weak memory, as demonstrated in the Tunis/Carthage confusion, and then turns the phrase around so that it refers to the short time Gonzalo will be remembered by others after he is dead.

240   *Professes to persuade* (in his role as councillor)

246–7 *Ambition cannot pierce ... discovery there.* To come by the throne of Naples, Antonio implies, would be to

rise so high that Ambition itself would doubt the pos-
sibility of discovering anything to achieve beyond it.

251-4 *Ten leagues beyond man's life ... rough and razorable.*
Antonio's desire to overcome Sebastian's hereditary
sloth as quickly as possible leads him to an extra-
ordinary set of exaggerations. They have just left
Tunis themselves, but he claims it is so distant that a
man might journey a whole lifetime and not get nearer
than thirty miles to it before he died, that only a
messenger who travelled with the speed of the sun
could inform Claribel that she was the heir of Naples
before many years had passed of Sebastian's rule.

255 *cast.* The initial meaning, 'cast on shore', transforms
itself into a theatrical image in the next two lines.
Prospero had used an image of this kind to describe
Antonio's usurpation to Miranda (I.2.107–8); now
Antonio unconsciously adopts the same terms to urge
Sebastian to a parallel act.

258 *discharge* theatrical performance

270-71 *could make | A chough of as deep chat* could train a
jackdaw to speak like him

275 *Tender* regard

278 *feuter* more becomingly

281-3 *If 'twere a kibe ... in my bosom.* If conscience produced
physical symptoms, like a sore heel, it would be
necessary to relieve it somehow. As it is, Antonio feels
no discomfort.

283-5 *Twenty consciences ... ere they molest.* This characteristic, and odd, Shakespearian image pattern occurs
in other plays: *Hamlet*, III.2.65, and *Antony and
Cleopatra*, IV.12.21.

289 *doing thus.* Antonio makes a mock gesture of stabbing.

290 *wink* sleep

294 *tell the clock* agree to

302-4 *My master through his art ... to keep them living.*
Ariel's actual words here are heard by the audience
only.

329   *Heavens keep him from these beasts.* Gonzalo presumably has his suspicions about Antonio and Sebastian, and there may be a deliberate ambiguity here.

II.2.3   *inch-meal* inch by inch

5   *urchin-shows* (apparitions, perhaps in the form of hedgehogs)

6   *like a firebrand* like a will-o'-the-wisp

9   *mow* grimace

18   *bear off* ward off. Trinculo is described in the Folio list of characters as 'a jester', but he is very difficult indeed to fit into that impressive succession of professional fools which runs from *As You Like It* to *King Lear*. He fulfils none of the functions associated with this character-type in plays written before *The Tempest*: he is not a truth-teller, a kind of Chorus character, nor does he provide any standard of wit in the play. As markedly inferior to Stephano in energy and invention as Sebastian is to Antonio, he seems to represent in this play Shakespeare's abandonment of a dramatic device which it had once been worth his while to exploit. It is interesting that both he and his fellow, Stephano, invariably speak prose as opposed to the verse of Caliban. There is a judgement implied here in the language which Shakespeare gives to his monster and to the two products of civilization, even as there is in the prose-speaking of Antonio and Sebastian.

21   *bombard* leather jug

26   *poor-John* salted hake

28   *and had but this fish painted.* Trinculo sees himself as exhibiting Caliban for cash at a fair, as a freak. A painting of the monster outside the booth would allure customers.

30   *make a man* make a man's fortune (with a quibble on *make* in the sense of 'be equivalent to')

31   *doit* coin of very small value

38   *gaberdine* cloak

40   *dregs.* Trinculo clings to his image of the black cloud as a wine jug.

45   *swabber* (seaman who washed down the decks)

55   *Do not torment me!* Trinculo is shaking with fear, a reaction which Caliban mistakes for the prelude to persecution by one of Prospero's agents.

60   *on four legs.* Stephano adjusts the 'two legs' of the saying to fit the phenomenon before him.

61   *at'* at his

67–9   *If I can recover him . . . on neat's leather.* Like Trinculo, Stephano's first reaction to the seemingly marvellous is to plan how to cash in on it. Characteristically, however, he is more energetic and practical in thinking of actually transporting Caliban to Naples – not simply indulging in a fantasy about his potential value there.

75–6   *I will not take too much for him.* This is a somewhat oblique way of saying he will not consider any sum, no matter how great, more than his monster is worth.

82   *cat.* This probably refers to the proverb: 'Ale will make a cat speak.'

97   *I have no long spoon.* This alludes to the proverb: 'He who sups with the devil must have a long spoon.'

104   *siege* excrement

         mooncalf monster (with the suggestion that the influence of the moon was responsible for this abnormal birth)

114   *an if* if

136   *when time was* once upon a time. Settlers in the New World frequently beguiled credulous natives with tales of this kind.

138   *thee, and thy dog, and thy bush.* The Man in the Moon was banished there, with his dog, for gathering brushwood on a Sunday.

145   *I'll show thee every fertile inch o'th'island.* Even as the conspiracy of Antonio and Sebastian against Alonso

is a repetition of Antonio's former treachery to Prospero, so Caliban here repeats to Stephano the same offers he had made to Prospero twelve years before.

148 *when's* when his

164 *crabs* crab-apples

165 *pignuts* groundnuts

169 *scamels*. Unexplained, and possibly a corruption in the text. It is possible that Caliban is referring to an edible species of rock-nesting bird (the godwit), or else to a shell-fish.

176 *No more dams.* Caliban has provided Prospero and Miranda with fish for their table by building dams in the island's streams to catch them. It is one of the unexplained, given facts of the play that, powerful though he is as a magician, Prospero nonetheless depends upon the manual labour of Caliban for the simplest necessities of life.

179 *trenchering* wooden plates

181 *get a new man!* (a drunkenly contemptuous injunction to the absent Prospero)

III.1.1–2 *There be some sports … in them sets off* some sports involve a certain amount of physical discomfort, but the pleasure derived from the exercise compensates for this

6 *quickens* gives life to

11 *sore injunction* stern command

12–13 *such baseness | Had never like executor* a task so mean was never performed by so noble a being

15 *Most busy lest.* This is the most famous textual crux in *The Tempest*. The present edition reproduces the Folio reading without attempt at emendation. The sense in any case seems clear. Ferdinand has paused momentarily in his task of piling logs in order to reflect upon Miranda. At the words 'I forget', he resumes his task,

commenting as he does so that he is really busiest when apparently most idle, because his mind in these moments is wholly occupied by thoughts of his love.

19   *'Twill weep* (by exuding resin)

31-2   *Poor worm . . . visitation shows it.* Prospero speaks of Miranda's love here as something caught involuntarily, like the plague. He puns on the word *visitation* in the sense of an epidemic, not simply Miranda's visit to Ferdinand. It is not the most cheerful way of describing a romantic attachment and it serves to stress Prospero's distance from the ecstasies of the lovers themselves.

34   *When you are by at night.* Ferdinand has not, of course, spent a night on the island. His statement here, with its sense of a time span greater than the play actually affords, gives the illusion that he has loved Miranda for longer than in fact he has, that events normally requiring days of development have unfolded within hours, or even minutes, of essentially magical time.

37   *hest* command

     Admired Miranda. Miranda's name itself means 'admirable', or 'to be wondered at'.

45   *owed* owned

46   *put it to the foil* defeated it (with the sense also of a contrast in which defect cancels out virtue)

53   *skill-less of* ignorant of

57-9   *But I prattle . . . therein do forget.* See Introduction, pages 30-31.

59   *condition* rank

63   *blow* contaminate

66-7   *and for your sake | Am I this patient log-man.* Gallantly, Ferdinand has in his own mind converted the ignominious task Prospero has set him into a service which he performs in order to win his lady. In so doing, he has stumbled unconsciously upon the truth of the situation.

69   *event* outcome

70–71   *If hollowly ... to mischief* if I am insincere, may the best good fortune coming to me turn to bad

79   *want* lack

80–81   *And all the more it seeks to hide itself ... it shows.* The imagery here is of a secret pregnancy. Sexual allusion of this kind hardly seems appropriate to Miranda, but Shakespeare is frequently concerned in the last plays that his verse should suggest the essential nature of the situation rather than the characteristics of the speaker's mind. Ideas of fertility and increase are central to this marriage (see the masque in Act IV) and they are foreshadowed here, beginning with Prospero's 'breeds' in line 76.

87   *And I thus humble ever.* Ferdinand kneels to promise his devotion.

96   *appertaining* related to this

III.2.2–3   *bear up and board 'em* (a phrase from sea-warfare, converted here into an exhortation to drink)

16   *he's no standard.* Caliban is too drunk to stand upright. Hence Trinculo's pun on a term intended by Stephano to mean 'standard-bearer'.

18–19   *Nor go neither ... say nothing neither.* Stephano's attempt to give a military dignity to his relation with Caliban is continually being deflated by Trinculo, here through a series of puns the secondary meanings of which are 'to make water' and the like.

25   *case* fit state
            deboshed debauched

32   *natural* idiot

35   *the next tree.* Stephano is proposing to hang Trinculo from it.

48   *in's* in his

63   *What a pied ninny ... patch.* Caliban refers to Trinculo's parti-coloured and patched dress as a jester.

67   *quick freshes* running streams of fresh water

70   *stockfish* dried cod, beaten before cooking

80   *murrain* plague affecting cattle

91   *paunch* stab in the belly

92   *weasand* wind-pipe

94   *sot* fool

97   *utensils* household furnishings

101   *nonpareil* paragon

111   *Excellent.* Uttered, presumably, in a sulky tone of voice, which prompts Stephano's subsequent attempt to make amends.

118   *troll the catch* sing out the catch. A catch is a part-song in which everyone sings the same melody, the second singer beginning the first line as the man who started the song moves on to the second, and so on.

119   *while-ere* a little time ago

122   *Flout 'em and scout 'em* (in effect, 'sneer at them and deride them')

125   (stage direction) *tabor* (a small drum worn at the side)

127-8   *played by the picture of Nobody* (probably a reference to contemporary pictures of a man with arms, legs, and a head but no body)

132-3   *He that dies . . . Mercy upon us !* Stephano is aware of the necessity of making a better showing than the terrified Trinculo before his servant-monster, but he is close to collapse.

154   *Wilt come?* (presumably addressed to Caliban)

.3.1   *By 'r lakin* by our Ladykin (the Virgin Mary)

3   *Through forthrights and meanders* through paths sometimes straight, sometimes winding

6   *attached* seized

15   *throughly* thoroughly

18   (stage direction) *Prospero on the top.* This stage direction may refer to an upper stage, in any case to a playing area above the level on which Alonso and his companions stand.

21   *kind keepers* guardian angels

22   *A living drollery* (a puppet-show in which the participants are real and not wooden figures)

24   *phoenix' throne.* The mythical phoenix was thought to dwell in Arabia and to be enthroned upon a single tree of a unique species. The phoenix itself was unique, only one bird existing at a time. The new phoenix sprang, miraculously, from the ashes of the funeral pyre which consumed the body of its predecessor. See Shakespeare's poem 'The Phoenix and the Turtle'.

26   *want credit* need believing

31-5   *For certes, these are people . . . nay, almost any.* It is characteristic of Gonzalo that he should be impressed by the gracious manners of Prospero's servants, not simply by their monstrous shapes. Again, he does not see the same thing that the wicked lords see.

37   *muse* wonder at. Alonso's concurrence with Gonzalo's judgement here serves to separate him further from Antonio and Sebastian.

40   *Praise in departing* save your commendation for the end

49   *Each putter-out of five for one.* Elizabethan travellers sometimes coined money from their exploits by depositing a given sum in London on departure, to be repaid five-fold if they returned safely and with proof of having actually been to the remote places for which they set out.

53   (stage direction) *a quaint device* (some ingenious mechanism, designed to surprise the theatre audience as much as the characters on the stage)

55-83   *That hath to instrument this lower world . . . clear life ensuing.* Ariel's speech is contorted and knotty in a fashion characteristic of Prospero. The style reminds the audience that Prospero is in fact the 'author' of this little play-within-the-play and responsible for the lines the harpy speaks. Ariel is saying that destiny uses the lower, or sublunary, world as its instrument. Like his claim that the island is uninhabited (line 58), this

view of the retributive function of Destiny is a fiction.
See Introduction, page 43.

60 *suchlike valour* the irrational courage of madness

65 *still-closing waters* waters which flow together again as
soon as divided

66 *dowle* small feather

67 *like* also

68 *massy* heavy

72 *requit* avenged

78 *Lingering perdition* slow ruin

80–83 *whose wraths . . . clear life ensuing* to escape the just
retribution of these powers, repentance and a blameless
future life is the only remedy. Otherwise, in this lonely
place, they will have their revenge.

83 (stage direction) *mocks and mows* (a derisive pantomime)

85 *devouring.* Harpies were noted for their voracious
appetites. Prospero's remark suggests that the 'quaint
device' with which the banquet disappeared included
an effect by which Ariel in this role appeared to devour
it himself.

86 *bated* left out

87–8 *good life | And observation strange.* As director of the
little show, Prospero praises his spirit actors for the
convincing nature of their performance and for their
careful execution of their parts.

89 *several kinds* individual parts

95–6 *I'th'name of something . . . strange stare.* Only the three
men of sin have heard Ariel's words, and even for
them the accusation seems to have proceeded in-
distinctly from sea and wind rather than from Ariel
himself, or at least this is how they remember it in their
distraction. Gonzalo and the other lords have heard
nothing.

101 *bass my trespass* (provide the bass, or ground, in the
whole harmony of accusing sound)

110 *ecstasy* frenzy

IV.1.3   *a third of mine own life*. What the other two-thirds are
is conjectural. Prospero may mean his dukedom and his
studies; he may mean that the twelve years spent on
Miranda's education has represented one-third of his
adult life. Essentially, the remark is enigmatic. Its
curious precision invites speculation but refuses
enlightenment. See Introduction, page 15.

5   *tender* offer

7   *strangely* wonderfully

9   *boast her off* boast about her (with a slight sense,
increased by the suggestion of a foot-race in the next
lines, of a competition)

11   *halt* limp

12   *Against* against the word of

16   *sanctimonious* holy

18   *aspersion* sprinkling, as of rain or dew. The whole
passage prefigures the fertility theme of the masque,
marriage being compared to the natural cycle of the
seasons.

23   *Hymen* (Roman god of marriage, usually represented
carrying a torch)

26   *opportune* (accent on the second syllable)

27   *Our worser genius can* one's bad angel can make

29   *edge* keen delight

30–31   *When I shall think . . . kept chained below* when the day
that divides me from the marriage-bed will seem so
long that I shall think the horses of the sun-god are
lame, or else that night is detained as a prisoner in the
lower world

37   *rabble* (spirits inferior to Ariel)

41   *vanity* show (with a slightly self-deprecating tone)

42   *Presently* immediately

43   *with a twink* in a twinkling

50   *conceive* understand

51   *Look thou be true*. Neither Ferdinand nor Miranda has
seen Ariel, nor heard Prospero's conversation with
him. They have been preoccupied with each other.

Prospero, turning back to the lovers at this point, presumably catches them in an embrace sufficiently passionate to arouse his fears.

55–6 *The white cold virgin snow ... of my liver.* Ferdinand appears to be saying that his consciousness of Miranda's chastity and innocence, as she rests in his arms, keeps his passion within proper bounds. The liver was thought of by Elizabethans as the source of sexual desire.

57–8 *Bring a corollary, | Rather than want a spirit* bring too many spirits, if need be, rather than too few

58 *pertly* briskly

59 *Be silent.* Silence was thought necessary for the success of magical operations. See lines 126–7.
(stage direction) *Iris.* She was goddess of the rainbow and one of the messengers of the gods. See line 71.

60–138 *Ceres, most bounteous ... country footing.* The verse of the masque is set off from that of the play proper by its formality and deliberate artifice. It is filled with archaic or uncommon words and invokes a deliberately unreal, remote, mythological world. At the same time, it contrives to admit glimpses of a genuine English countryside, and to maintain a delicate balance between those ideas of warmth and increase appropriate to a betrothal celebration and a stress on chastity and restraint. Unlike Ariel's speech as the harpy in Act III, the words of the masque do not seem to be Prospero's, although they reflect his preoccupations.

60 *Ceres* (goddess responsible for the fertility of the earth). Her part is played by Ariel.
leas meadows

61 *fetches* vetches (a kind of forage)

63 *stover* (a kind of winter forage, on which sheep live when summer is over)

64 *pionèd and twillèd brims.* These two adjectives are obscure in meaning, though it seems likely that they have something to do with eroded river banks which

have been artificially reinforced, possibly by means of a woven barricade of branches.

65 *spongy*. The word suggests the quality of spring earth saturated with rain.

hest command

68 *pole-clipt* (probably a vineyard where the vines twine around and so seem to embrace their supporting poles)

70 *air* take the air

the queen o'th'sky (Juno herself)

74 *peacocks* (the birds sacred to Juno, here described as drawing her chariot through the skies)

amain at full speed

(stage direction) *Juno descends*. Juno's entrance seems to be signalized surprisingly early in the text, considering that her presence is not recognized by the other characters in the masque until line 101, and she does not speak until line 103. It is likely, however, that her descent was slow and deliberately impressive. Probably, she remained in her airy chariot, presiding silently over the conversation between Iris and Ceres from a position a little above their heads, until line 101, when her chariot was lowered to the stage and she alighted from it.

80–81 *And with each end of thy blue bow ... unshrubbed down* (one end of the rainbow rests in wooded country, the other in bare downlands)

85 *estate* bestow

89 *The means that dusky Dis my daughter got*. Proserpina, Ceres's daughter, was abducted by Dis, the ruler of the underworld.

90 *scandalled* scandalous

93 *Paphos* (in Cyprus, a favourite abode of Venus and the centre of her worship)

94 *Dove-drawn* (doves were sacred to Venus, as peacocks to Juno, and drew her chariot)

94–7 *Here thought they to have done ... torch be lighted*. In this piece of mischief averted, and in the reference

168

earlier to the rape of Proserpina, lies the explanation of Iris's and Ceres's hostility to Venus and Cupid. The latter are conceived of as the deities of lawless love, of wantonness outside wedlock, as opposed to Juno who is patroness of marriage and ceremony, and Ceres, patroness of an ordered fertility linking human love with the cycle of the seasons.

98   *Mars's hot minion is returned again* Venus, the lustful mistress of the god Mars, has returned (to Paphos)

99   *waspish-headed* peevish

100   *sparrows.* Sparrows, also associated with Venus, were symbols of lechery.

101   *And be a boy right out* and be an ordinary boy

110   *foison* abundance

114–15 *Spring come to you . . . end of harvest.* Ceres wishes for the lovers a year without winter, in which the abundance of autumn flows without interruption into the new promise of spring.

120–22 *by mine art . . . My present fancies.* The masque is a fantasy created by the spirits themselves upon the preoccupations of Prospero's mind (his *present fancies*), which he is able to project to them through his art.

123   *wondered* to be wondered at

128   *windring* winding and wandering. The word appears to be Shakespeare's invention.

130   *crisp* rippling

138   *country footing* rustic dance
      (stage direction) *heavily* dejectedly

139–42 *I had forgot . . . Is almost come.* See Introduction, pages 27–30, for a discussion of Prospero's possible reasons for taking Caliban's conspiracy so seriously.

142   *Avoid* begone

144   *works him strongly* affects him greatly

145   *distempered* out of temper

150   *into thin air.* Spirits were thought to become visible through a thickening of the airy element of which they

were composed. A resolution back to *thin air* meant, therefore, their disappearance from sight.

154   *it inherit* occupy it

156   *rack* a shred of cloud. The word also had a technical application to the stage clouds often used in court masques to dissolve a scene. This secondary meaning reinforces the underlying sense in Prospero's description of the dissolution of the world as being like that of some great court performance.

158   *rounded with a sleep* (at either end of life, before birth and after death, there is only sleep)

167   *When I presented Ceres*. This edition presumes that 'presented' means played the part of, not simply acted as stage manager for. Ariel appears in a number of disguises in the course of *The Tempest*; it seems reasonable to suppose that here, as in the show in Act III, he takes part in the performance itself.

170   *varlets* ruffians

174–5   *bending | Towards* pursuing

176   *unbacked* unbroken

177   *Advanced* lifted up

179   *calf-like*. The imagery shifts here from colts to calves, while continuing to insist upon the brutish, animal nature of the three conspirators.

180   *goss* gorse

182   *filthy mantled* covered with scum

186   *trumpery* showy rubbish

187   *stale* decoy

193   *line* lime tree

197   *Jack* jack-o'-lantern, or will-o'-the-wisp (with a subsidiary sense of knave)

206   *hoodwink this mischance* blind this misfortune, rendering it incapable of further mischief (with a subsidiary sense of putting it out of sight)

222–3   *O King Stephano . . . a wardrobe here is for thee*. The sight of the glistering apparel reminds Trinculo of a popular ballad also mentioned in *Othello*: 'King

Stephen was and a worthy peer; | His breeches cost him but a crown.'

It is remarkable that all three of the conspiracies in *The Tempest*, that of Antonio and Sebastian in Act II, that of Alonso and Antonio as Prospero describes it to Miranda in Act I, and this one, involve the imagery of the stage. Here, the theatrical association is worked out in terms of costume, the most superficial and obvious part of any royal impersonation and therefore appropriate to Stephano's nature and his attempt.

226   *frippery* (a place where second-hand clothes are sold)

231   *luggage* useless and encumbering junk. Caliban, who has been sobered by his wetting in the pond, is suddenly the only one of the conspirators with any sense at all.

235-8   *Mistress line, is not this my jerkin? ... a bald jerkin.* *Jerkin* is a short, close-fitting jacket. The jokes here on the word *line* depend on the notion that sailors who crossed the equator (*line*) lost their hair from scurvy.

239   *line and level* (another quibble, meaning 'according to rule')

239-40   *an't like your grace* if it please you

244   *pass of pate* sally of wit. Stephano's ludicrous imitation of royalty seems to increase as he costumes himself for the part.

245   *lime* bird-lime (a sticky substance to which Trinculo imagines the finery adhering)

248   *barnacles* (a variety of goose popularly supposed to begin life as a shellfish)

260   *dry convulsions* (obscure, but possibly related to some contemporary medical theory about pains caused by an insufficiency of liquids in the body)

261   *aged cramps* cramps such as old people have

262   *pard or cat o'mountain* leopard or panther

267   (stage direction) *Exeunt*. The F stage directions here and at the beginning of V.1 indicate that Prospero and Ariel should exit and then reappear immediately to

begin the next scene. In production, they are sometimes allowed to remain on stage. The quality of the verse seems to argue for the kind of short but decisive break that music between the Acts could provide.

V.1.2–3 *and time | Goes upright with his carriage.* There is so little left to do that time, relieved of most of his burden, walks upright and easily.

10 *weather-fends* protects from the weather

11 *till your release* until you liberate them

16–17 *like winter's drops | From eaves of reeds* like winter rain dripping from a thatched roof

18 *affections* feelings

21 *touch* a refined apprehension

23–4 *that relish ... | Passion as they* that (because like them I am mortal) feel passion even as they do

23 *relish* feel

24 *kindlier.* The word has the double sense of 'more sympathetically' and also more in accord with the human kinship Prospero shares with his victims, but not with the spirit Ariel.

28 *They being penitent.* At this point, Prospero cannot know how much of a change of heart Alonso, Antonio, and Sebastian will feel, but he adopts a hopeful attitude.

33–50 *Ye elves of hills, brooks ... By my so potent art.* Shakespeare seems to have derived this speech from the one Ovid gave to the sorceress Medea in the seventh book of the *Metamorphoses.* In Golding's translation of 1567, which it is thought Shakespeare used, the equivalent lines (265–77) are these:

> Ye airs and winds: ye elves of hills, of brooks, of woods alone,
> Of standing lakes, and of the night, approach ye every one.

172

Through help of whom (the crooked banks much
    wondering at the thing)
I have compelled streams to run clean backward to
    their spring.
By charms I make the calm seas rough, and make the
    rough seas plain,
And cover all the sky with clouds and chase them
    thence again.
By charms I raise and lay the winds, and burst the
    viper's jaw,
And from the bowels of the earth both stones and
    trees do draw.
Whole woods and forests I remove. I make the
    mountains shake,
And even the earth itself to groan and fearfully to
    quake.
I call up dead men from their graves, and thee, O
    lightsome moon,
I darken oft, though beaten brass abate thy peril
    soon.
Our sorcery dims the morning fair and darks the
    sun at noon.

36   *demi-puppets* fairies of doll or puppet-like size and
    appearance

37   *green, sour ringlets* fairy rings in the grass

39   *midnight mushrumps* mushrooms that appear overnight

39–40   *that rejoice | To hear the solemn curfew* (because the
    curfew bell releases them to 'that vast of night that
    they may work' (I.2.327), the period of a spirit's power)

45   *rifted* split
    Jove's stout oak. The oak tree was sacred to Jove.

47   *spurs* roots

50   *rough magic.* See Introduction, pages 27–30.

53   *their senses that* the senses of those whom

58–83   *A solemn air . . . would know me.* This whole speech,
    which alternates between direct address to Gonzalo,

Alonso, Sebastian, and Antonio and comment upon their appearance and slow return to normal consciousness, is not heard by the members of the court party. Not until line 111, in fact, does it become evident that any of them even see Prospero before them, let alone register what he says.

58–60 *A solemn air ... within thy skull.* Prospero's use of music as a cure for mental distraction is in accord with Renaissance belief.

63 *sociable to the show of thine* sympathetic to the appearance of yours

70–71 *I will pay thy graces |Home* I will requite your favours fully

76 *remorse* pity

85 *discase me* (of his magician's robes)

86 *sometime Milan* when I was Duke of Milan

96 *so, so, so.* These words seem to be uttered half-consciously under his breath while Ariel puts the finishing touches to his costume.

111 *Whe'er* whether

112 *trifle* trick of magic
abuse deceive

116 *crave* require

117 *An if this be at all* if this is actually happening

124 *subtleties.* There is a pun here on 'subtleties' as a kind of elaborate pastry, and so literally to be tasted.

129 *No.* Prospero has heard Sebastian's aside, presumably through his magic art. The same power of divination has, apparently, told him that Alonso is truly repentant although the other two 'men of sin' are not. His terse, one-word denial of Sebastian's theory here is meant to be cold and intimidating.

131–2 *I do forgive | Thy rankest fault.* Seneca, in his essay, 'On Anger', had declared that 'It is the part of a great man to despise injuries and it is one kind of revenge to neglect a man as not worth it.' This, rather than any spirit of Christian charity, appears to be the sentiment reflected in Prospero's pardon of his brother.

139   *woe* sorry

145   *supportable* (accent on the first syllable)

154   *admire* wonder

155   *devour* (with a sense of 'open-mouthed' astonishment)

156   *do offices of truth* function truthfully

171   (stage direction) *Here Prospero discovers Ferdinand and Miranda, playing at chess.* It is characteristic of *The Tempest* that the discovery of the lovers should be made in so theatrical a fashion that the members of the court party cannot tell at first if what they see is real, or only another 'subtlety', one of the deceiving shows of the island.

       discovers reveals

172–5   *Sweet lord, you play me false ... call it fair play.* For an instant, the lovers do not notice the company before whom they have suddenly been revealed. They continue, oblivious, in their own private world. The interchange in itself is not easy to understand. Miranda's *false* surely cannot be interpreted to mean that Ferdinand is cheating at chess – something which the nature of the game makes virtually impossible in any case. Presumably, she is reproaching him gently for some threatening move on the board. His hyperbolic assertion that he would not play her false for the whole world she then proceeds to deflate (much as Emilia does in *Othello*, IV.3.67–77) with the remark that for such a stake as a score of kingdoms he certainly would do so, and that she, in her love for him, would call it fair.

186   *eld'st* longest

187–8   *Is she the goddess.* Alonso makes the same mistake about Miranda that Ferdinand had made when he first saw her in Act I. His question demonstrates how far the members of the court party still are from feeling certain of reality, despite the revelations of Prospero.

201–13 *Look down, you gods . . . was his own.* See Introduction, pages 36–7.

224 *yare* ready (for sea)

232 *several* various

238 *On a trice* in an instant

240 *moping* dazedly

244 *conduct* conductor of

244–5 *Some oracle | Must rectify our knowledge.* Even at this late stage, no one thinks of turning to Prospero for explanations.

247–8 *At picked leisure . . . single I'll resolve you* I myself will explain to you, in ways that shall seem probable, what has passed

256 *Every man shift for all the rest.* Stephano has managed, unwittingly, to give an altruistic twist to a saying intended to mean the opposite.

259 *true spies* accurate observers

261 *Setebos* (the god worshipped by Caliban's mother Sycorax)

264–6 *What things are these . . . no doubt marketable.* See Introduction, pages 38–9. Significantly, Antonio and Sebastian react to their first sight of Caliban exactly as their inferiors, Stephano and Trinculo, had. They speculate on his possible market value.

267 *badges* (identifying insignia indicating to whose service they belonged)

271 *And deal in her command without her power.* Sycorax could exercise some of the authority of the moon herself, without possessing her full power. It is presumably a situation like that exemplified in her treatment of Ariel as described in I.2.289–91. She could summon him, but could not force him to obey 'her earthy and abhorred commands', could imprison him in the cloven pine, but not undo her own spell.

275–6 *This thing of darkness I | Acknowledge mine.* Some commentators on the play have argued from this line that *The Tempest* is essentially an interior drama in which Caliban represents the dark, animal side of Prospero. More probably, it is simply Prospero's responsibility for a creature he has failed to alter which he accepts here.

281–4   *this pickle ... not fear fly-blowing*. Alonso uses the word *pickle* in the sense of predicament. Trinculo, more literally, interprets it as the process of soaking meat in alcohol to preserve it. He is, he feels, so well saturated that the flies will not come near him.

295–8   *I'll be wise hereafter ... worship this dull fool*. Caliban at least gets further than either Antonio or Sebastian in the direction of self-knowledge and understanding of the situation, although his primary achievement seems to be the recognition that his new masters were unworthy of respect.

312   *Every third thought shall be my grave*. See Introduction, page 16.

314   *Take* captivate

316–17   *shall catch | Your royal fleet far off* enable you to overtake your royal fleet on the way back to Naples

Epilogue

For comment on the epilogue generally, see Introduction pages 49–51.

9   *bands* bonds

10   *of your good hands* (with your applause, the noise of which will break the spell)

11   *Gentle breath* (favourable comment on the play)

16   *prayer* (this appeal to the audience)

AN ACCOUNT OF THE TEXT

THERE is only one text for *The Tempest*, that of the Folio (F) of 1623. It is the first play in the volume and it seems to have been prepared with particular accuracy and care, as though Shakespeare's editors were determined that the first impression received by the reader should be a favourable one. The text is unusually short, and it is sometimes argued that the play as it appears in F represents a revised version of a longer original. None of these revision theories are convincing. Probably, *The Tempest* was transcribed from a playhouse copy by Ralph Crane, who was attached to Shakespeare's company as a scrivener. The result, neatly and intelligently divided into Acts and scenes, equipped with a list of characters and meticulously punctuated throughout, stands as perhaps the cleanest of Shakespeare's texts. There is a famous crux at III.1.15; some of Caliban's verse is set as prose in F, and there are indications that the prose he does speak, in some instances, was originally cast as blank verse. Otherwise only a few minor errors seem to have crept in.

COLLATIONS

Alterations to F of any consequence are listed below, with F's reading on the right of the bracket.

I

The Characters in the Play] (In F this list appears at the end of the play, and includes the indication on setting 'an vn-inhabited Island'.)

I.1. 48–9   Set her two courses! Off to sea again!] set her
two courses off to Sea againe

I.2. 201   lightnings] Lightning

      212   Then all afire with me. The King's son Ferdi-
nand] Then all a fire with me the Kings sonne
Ferdinand

      282   she] he

      380   the burden bear] beare the burthen

II.1. 18–19 When every grief is entertained that's offered, |
Comes to th'entertainer] When euery greefe is
entertaind, | That's offer'd comes to th'enter-
tainer.

       38–9   ANTONIO ... SEBASTIAN] (The speakers are
reversed in F.)

II.2. 114–16 These be fine things ... kneel to him] (Set as
prose in F.)

       157–61 I'll show thee ... | Thou wondrous man] (Set as
prose in F.)

       164–9   I prithee, let me bring thee ... go with me?]
(Set as prose in F.)

III.1.   2   sets] set

III.2. 22–3   How does thy honour ... he is not valiant] (Set
as prose in F.)

        122–4   Flout 'em and scout 'em, | And scout 'em and
flout 'em! | Thought is free.] *Flout'em, and
cout'em: and skowt'em, and flout'em, | Thought is
free.*

III.3.   30   islanders] Islands

IV.1.   9   off] of

        13   gift] guest

        74   Her] here

        193   hang them on] hang on them

        231   Let't] let's

V.1.   60   boiled] boile

        72   Didst] Did

        75   entertained] entertaine

        82   lies] ly

V.1.   248 Which shall be shortly, single I'll resolve you]
            (Which shall be shortly single) I'le resolue you

2

The stage directions for *The Tempest* are unusually full and
elaborate. They may be Shakespeare's work; they may possibly
have been added by Ralph Crane. In the present edition all
asides or indications of the character to whom a particular
speech is addressed are additions to the original text. Other
additions or alterations made in this edition are listed below,
within brackets.

I.1.   33 Exit [Exeunt Gonzalo and the other nobles]
        50 [Exeunt]
        58 [Exit Boatswain]
        60 Exit [with Antonio]
I.2.   186 [Miranda sleeps]
       304 Exit [Ariel]
II.1. 193 [All sleep except Alonso, Sebastian, and Antonio]
       201 [Alonso sleeps. Exit Ariel]
       311 [awakes]
       312 [The others awake]
II.2.   36 [Thunder]
        40 Enter Stephano singing [a bottle in his hand]
        44 Drinkes. Sings. [He drinks and then sings]
        84 [He gives Caliban wine]
        92 [Caliban drinks]
       127 [He gives him wine]
       140 [Caliban drinks]
III.1. 15 and Prospero [at a distance, unseen]
        91 Exeunt [Ferdinand and Miranda in different
           directions]
III.2. 76 [He strikes Trinculo]
III.3. 18 Solemn and strange music . . . they depart [This
           follows 'As when they are fresh' in F.]

III.3.   61 [Alonso, Sebastian, and the others draw their
                swords]
         104 [Exit]
         105 [Exeunt Antonio and Sebastian]
IV.1.   124 Juno and Ceres whisper . . . Iris on employment
                [This follows line 127 in F.]
         163 Exit [Exeunt Ferdinand and Miranda]
         258 [Caliban, Stephano, and Trinculo are driven out]
V.1.   179 [He comes forward, and kneels]
         253 [Exit Ariel]
         300 [Exeunt Caliban, Stephano, and Trinculo]

THE MUSIC

For two of the songs in *The Tempest* we have settings which may have been used in performances during Shakespeare's lifetime. They first appeared in Dr John Wilson's collection, *Cheerful Ayres or Ballads*, in 1659, and are there attributed to Robert Johnson. He was appointed lutenist to King James in 1604, and composed for the Court and for the public theatres. He died in 1633. The following transcriptions give the songs as published, with a bass accompaniment. They are printed with lute accompaniment in *English Lute Songs* (Second Series, volume 17, edited by Ian Spink), and arrangements for voice and piano were made by Anthony Lewis (Lyrebird Press, Paris, 1936). There is a recording by James Bowman (counter-tenor) and Robert Spencer (lute): 'Elizabethan Lute Songs', HMV HQS 1281.

1. 'Full fathom five' (I.2.397).

2. 'Where the bee sucks' (V.1.88).

A Dance

In a British Museum manuscript (Add. MS. 10444) of masque music one of the dances (No. 62) is labelled 'The Tempest'. It is attributed in the British Museum Catalogue to Robert Johnson. It may possibly have been written for the play and intended for either the Reapers' Dance (IV.1.138) or the dance of the shapes (III.3.18).

READ MORE IN PENGUIN

In every corner of the world, on every subject under the sun, Penguin represents quality and variety – the very best in publishing today.

For complete information about books available from Penguin – including Puffins, Penguin Classics and Arkana – and how to order them, write to us at the appropriate address below. Please note that for copyright reasons the selection of books varies from country to country.

In the United Kingdom: Please write to *Dept. EP, Penguin Books Ltd, Bath Road, Harmondsworth, West Drayton, Middlesex UB7 0DA*

In the United States: Please write to *Consumer Sales, Penguin USA, P.O. Box 999, Dept. 17109, Bergenfield, New Jersey 07621-0120*. VISA and MasterCard holders call 1-800-253-6476 to order Penguin titles

In Canada: Please write to *Penguin Books Canada Ltd, 10 Alcorn Avenue, Suite 300, Toronto, Ontario M4V 3B2*

In Australia: Please write to *Penguin Books Australia Ltd, P.O. Box 257, Ringwood, Victoria 3134*

In New Zealand: Please write to *Penguin Books (NZ) Ltd, Private Bag 102902, North Shore Mail Centre, Auckland 10*

In India: Please write to *Penguin Books India Pvt Ltd, 706 Eros Apartments, 56 Nehru Place, New Delhi 110 019*

In the Netherlands: Please write to *Penguin Books Netherlands bv, Postbus 3507, NL-1001 AH Amsterdam*

In Germany: Please write to *Penguin Books Deutschland GmbH, Metzlerstrasse 26, 60594 Frankfurt am Main*

In Spain: Please write to *Penguin Books S. A., Bravo Murillo 19, 1° B, 28015 Madrid*

In Italy: Please write to *Penguin Italia s.r.l., Via Felice Casati 20, I–20124 Milano*

In France: Please write to *Penguin France S. A., 17 rue Lejeune, F–31000 Toulouse*

In Japan: Please write to *Penguin Books Japan, Ishikiribashi Building, 2-5-4, Suido, Bunkyo-ku, Tokyo 112*

In South Africa: Please write to *Longman Penguin Southern Africa (Pty) Ltd, Private Bag X08, Bertsham 2013*

RSC
ROYAL
SHAKESPEARE
COMPANY

The Royal Shakespeare Company today is probably one of the best-known theatre companies in the world, playing regularly to audiences of more than a million people a year. The RSC has three theatres in Stratford-upon-Avon, the Royal Shakespeare Theatre, the Swan Theatre and The Other Place, and two theatres in London's Barbican Centre, the Barbican Theatre and The Pit. The Company also has an annual season in Newcastle-upon-Tyne and regularly undertakes tours throughout the UK and overseas.

Find out more about the RSC and its current repertoire by joining the Company's mailing list. Not only will you receive advance information of all the Company's activities, but also priority booking, special ticket offers, copies of the RSC Magazine and special offers on RSC publications and merchandise.

If you would like to receive details of the Company's work and an application form for the mailing list please write to:

RSC Membership Office
Royal Shakespeare Theatre
FREEPOST
Stratford-upon-Avon
CV37 6BR

or telephone: 01789 205301

READ MORE IN PENGUIN

CRITICAL STUDIES

Described by *The Times Educational Supplement* as 'admirable' and 'superb', Penguin Critical Studies is a specially developed series of critical essays on the major works of literature for use by students in universities, colleges and schools.

Titles published or in preparation include:

SHAKESPEARE

Antony and Cleopatra
As You Like It
Coriolanus
Henry IV Part 2
Hamlet
Julius Caesar
King Lear
The Merchant of Venice
A Midsummer Night's Dream
Much Ado About Nothing
Othello
Richard II
Richard III
Romeo and Juliet
Shakespeare – Text into Performance
Shakespeare's History Plays
The Tempest
Troilus and Cressida
Twelfth Night
The Winter's Tale

CHAUCER

Chaucer
The Pardoner's Tale
The Prologue to The
  Canterbury Tales

READ MORE IN PENGUIN

THE NEW PENGUIN SHAKESPEARE

All's Well That Ends Well	Barbara Everett
Antony and Cleopatra	Emrys Jones
As You Like It	H. J. Oliver
The Comedy of Errors	Stanley Wells
Coriolanus	G. R. Hibbard
Hamlet	T. J. B. Spencer
Henry IV, Part 1	P. H. Davison
Henry IV, Part 2	P. H. Davison
Henry V	A. R. Humphreys
Henry VI, Parts 1–3	Norman Sanders
(three volumes)	
Henry VIII	A. R. Humphreys
Julius Caesar	Norman Sanders
King John	R. L. Smallwood
King Lear	G. K. Hunter
Love's Labour's Lost	John Kerrigan
Macbeth	G. K. Hunter
Measure for Measure	J. M. Nosworthy
The Merchant of Venice	W. Moelwyn Merchant
The Merry Wives of Windsor	G. R. Hibbard
A Midsummer Night's Dream	Stanley Wells
Much Ado About Nothing	R. A. Foakes
The Narrative Poems	Maurice Evans
Othello	Kenneth Muir
Pericles	Philip Edwards
Richard II	Stanley Wells
Richard III	E. A. J. Honigmann
Romeo and Juliet	T. J. B. Spencer
The Sonnets *and* A Lover's Complaint	John Kerrigan
The Taming of the Shrew	G. R. Hibbard
The Tempest	Anne Barton
Timon of Athens	G. R. Hibbard
Troilus and Cressida	R. A. Foakes
Twelfth Night	M. M. Mahood
The Two Gentlemen of Verona	Norman Sanders
The Two Noble Kinsmen	N. W. Bawcutt
The Winter's Tale	Ernest Schanzer